IN SEARCH OF THE SEVEN COLORS

by
ANIL GIGA

CYNTOMEDIA CORPORATION

Pittsburgh, PA

ISBN #1-56315-314-9

Paperback Fiction
© Copyright 2004 Anil Giga
All Rights Reserved
First Printing — 2004
Library of Congress #2002113712

Request for information should be addressed to:

SterlingHouse Publisher, Inc.
7436 Washington Avenue
Pittsburgh, PA 15218
www.sterlinghousepublisher.com

SterlingHouse Publisher, Inc. is a company
of the CyntoMedia Corporation.

Book Designer: Beth Buckholtz
Cover Design: Eric C. Moresea — SterlingHouse Publisher, Inc.

Printed in Canada

Dedication

THIS BOOK IS DEDICATED TO:

Yasmin, my wife and soul mate. Her love lights my life, her nobility overcomes me.

Alkarim my son, a mountain eagle and a free spirit. He taught me the meaning of patience.

Alqaim my son, timeless wonder and hard to define. He is the soul of many things, who showed me the meaning of trust.

Aziza my daughter, who showed me the meaning of joy. A fragrance neither from the East nor West.

Our parents, who taught us the meaning of sacrifice. We honor them.

And to the one who knows.

The Origins of
'In Search of the Seven Colors'

The storm blew over our nest
Afflicting my love and soul mate
Smitten by the incurable winds of cancer
Our foundations were shaken.

In this time of turmoil and pain
At the depth of agony,
I went to a place
Few men go,
But many fall into.

A desolated alley
Barren and forsaken
So dark, I could not see,
Maybe it was hell
In this pit of despair did I sob,
searching for my soul.
It was here,
In the midst of crisis
That I found the rainbow.

"Rise up and take your place by my side" it said.
"How" I cried
"Write, for you and others" it responded.
So I wrote, for seven moons...

Introduction

Never has a generation entered a new millennium as unsure about itself as the one today. The new epoch brings with it the lure of prosperity, technology and rapid progress. The great changes that lie ahead will inevitably force stress and distress into our lives. This is the potent force that breaks up marriages, destroys families and creates conflicts at the workplace. The need to find a formula for balanced living, one that will allow our generation to survive and succeed, has never been more urgent.

This book contains the collective wisdom of the ancient Sufis who, over centuries of esoteric contemplation and detachment, were able to draw from the Akashic records* those blueprints that set forth for humanity a total approach to balanced living.

These blueprints, sought by man from the beginning of time, will enable you to achieve happiness, harmony and success. They are now in your hands, contained in the parable of Jonathan's journey...

*The Akashic records, sometimes referred to as the sacred template, contain the perennial knowledge of everything past, present and future.

Chapter 1

*"The Bird is flying on high and
its shadow is speeding on the earth.
Some fool begins to chase the shadow
running so far that he becomes exhausted."*[1]

Jonathan had a perfect life. He had married his childhood sweetheart, Crystal, and together they were raising two bright, loving children, Jasmin, seven, and Justin, eight. They lived in an upper middle-class suburb of Toronto. A Volvo and a Mercedes occupied the two-car garage of their modern mansion.

Jonathan spent as much time in New York, London and Paris as he did in Toronto. His position as the executive vice president of marketing for International Media Group, an advertising company with offices on three continents, required that he travel often.

At the age of forty-four, he was considered by most people to be wildly successful. A Harvard MBA alumnus, he was looked to as a role model by future graduates, and his career was studied as an example of achievement in business.

Jonathan had a perfect life. But all that was about to change—abruptly, permanently—on one warm day in early spring.

The date was May 5. After a series of weekend meetings with important clients overseas, Jonathan landed at the Toronto airport around noon. Quickly clearing customs and immigration, he began to scan the throngs of people waiting expectantly in the arrivals area for Crystal's beautiful face. Ordinarily, he would have taken a cab, but this time Crystal had insisted on picking him up. The thirty-minute ride home was filled with chitchat about the kids, the neighbors, family and friends. As they pulled into the driveway, Jonathan was deep in thought about what lay ahead for him at the office. He did not notice that the red roses by the front door had bloomed, nor did he see the U-haul trailer hitched to their second car.

"I'm going for a quick shower," Jonathan said over his shoulder as he began climbing the spiral staircase to their master bedroom.

"I put out some fresh towels for you," Crystal called up the stairwell. She turned toward the kitchen to get some coffee started. "Better make it strong," she whispered to herself, reaching for a dark roast.

When Jonathan came down, he was dressed for the office. He followed the aroma of freshly brewed coffee to the kitchen.

"I need to talk to you about something important," Crystal said in a soft voice, as Jonathan stood at the kitchen island stirring his coffee. Crystal poured herself a cup and as she looked up, their eyes met. Jonathan felt a sudden chill run up his spine.

"I'm leaving you, Jonathan," she said, with the sound of immense sadness in her voice. "I'm taking the children with me to my mother's as soon as they get home from school."

Jonathan stood, frozen in place, feeling that his legs were turning to rubber. Minutes passed. He felt as if he couldn't breathe. The room seemed to be revolving around him. He thought he might be sick. When finally he spoke, his voice sounded like a frightened child's. "Why are you doing this?" he blurted out. "I love you! I love the kids!"

Crystal kept a calm demeanor, although she could feel her heart racing. She responded gently. "I know you love us, but you love us as if we were your possessions. What part of our lives are you involved in? How often do the children see you? When we married we shared so many dreams about our life together, we had all those hopes and aspirations, and they're just not important to you anymore. It seems that the children and I are getting in your way, stifling you, keeping you from the only thing you care about: your career."

Jonathan stared blankly as Crystal continued. "Often I wonder what happened," she said. "We were going to live differently. We wanted to make a difference. Didn't we plan to build a family life based on spiritual values? What happened, Jonathan?"

"We need to have some time apart. I'm so unhappy, you know I am. We've talked about it numerous times." Big tears began to roll down her cheeks. "I feel we are drifting further and further apart," she said, gasping through her sobs. "Jonathan, you have not kept one promise you have made to me or the children," she cried, her inner anguish clearly audible now.

Jonathan was speechless; everything Crystal had said was familiar and had been discussed before. He heard the ring of truth in her words.

Crystal stood. She picked up her handbag, leaned over and kissed Jonathan on the cheek, and, wiping away her tears with the back of her hand, she said hoarsely, "Mrs. Peters is driving the kids today—they should be home by 3:30. I'll come by in the evening to pick them up."

Then she was gone.

Jonathan heard the door close. He sat by the island at the center of the kitchen, staring blankly at the clock. Two p.m. I'll be okay, he thought. If she wants to leave me, let her go. I don't need anyone. Then, he pictured Crystal at her mother's home in Brampton, some two hours away, and he sighed heavily.

At ten past three, the ringing of the phone awakened Jonathan. One side of his face and ear reddened by the awkward way in which he had fallen asleep where he sat at the kitchen island. He grabbed the receiver and held it to the other ear.

It was Mrs. Peters. The expression on Jonathan's face changed quickly from despondency to panic. Mrs. Peters had been in a car accident! Justin was fine, but Jasmin had been taken to the hospital. It didn't sound good. Jonathan slammed the receiver down, grabbed his jacket and nearly flew out the door. Behind the wheel of his Mercedes, he used one hand to call Crystal on the cell phone as he sped to the hospital.

When Dr. Miles arrived in the private waiting area, Crystal and Jonathan were sitting rigidly in two of the overstuffed armchairs. They clung anxiously to each word he said. "She will recover from her physical injuries," he told them. "However, our concern right now is that she is in a coma. We cannot tell how serious her head injuries are. We'll just have to wait and see."

"But will she be all right?" Crystal asked.

The doctor looked at Crystal; tears glistened on her tired face. "We will do everything we possibly can do," he said quietly.

4

"Is there anything that we can do?" Jonathan asked, then glanced away suddenly as he felt emotion welling up in his chest.

Dr. Miles looked at them gravely. "You could pray."

Crystal searched Jonathan's face for his reaction. His unease was apparent. He was not the type of person who sat back and did nothing. Praying meant giving up control.

"We have extended medical coverage through my job," Jonathan said. "I'm going to talk to the nurse about getting Jasmin into a private room. We'll get her the best care that money can buy." As they left the waiting room, Jonathan looked so solemn, Crystal nearly started crying again.

The next two nights were hard for both Jonathan and Crystal. The private room enabled Crystal to stay by Jasmin's side constantly. Justin was at his grandmother's, and Jonathan seemed to wander in a daze from home, to work, to the hospital, and back again.

On the third day, Jasmin emerged from the coma. Her first words were, "Where's Daddy?"

When Jonathan came by that afternoon, the relief on both his and Crystal's faces was visible. A great weight had lifted.

"Dr. Miles just left," Crystal said, wearing a smile on her lips and in her eyes. "Jasmin can come home tomorrow. She can't walk, but Dr. Miles was hopeful. Still there's no guarantee she ever will." Crystal's voice trembled.

Jonathan reached for Crystal's hand and held it tightly. "Things will be fine; Jasmin will be fine. You'll see," he said.

Crystal pulled her hand away with a sharp retort. "How?"

Jonathan was silent. The realization dawned on him that for once he was powerless.

Jonathan arrived home from work the next day, jumped into the shower and then changed. His routine lately had brought him home at four, and he was at the hospital by four-thirty. The red light on the phone was flashing, so he pressed the playback button to check his messages while running his electric shaver over his face. He stopped suddenly, stared at the mirror, switched off the shaver and put down the phone. Crystal had left a message; she had picked up Jasmin and would be at her mother's, in Brampton. As the steam on the mirror began to clear, a distorted image peered back at him. His ragged-looking face seemed unfamiliar.

The evening went by slowly. As he sat alone in the living room, engrossed in his thoughts, the phone rang numerous times, but Jonathan stayed glued to the sofa. Darkness crept into the room, bringing a chill made visible by his breath condensing into white wisps. By eight in the morning, the living room had once again brightened as the sun glared through the window. Jonathan awoke and rose shakily from the sofa. He picked up the phone on his way upstairs. By the time he had finished telling his secretary that he wouldn't be coming in, he was about to fall into bed.

Jonathan slept the whole day in the same way as he had at night, frequently waking, thinking, This is a bad dream, I'll wake up and the nightmare will end. But no matter how many times he fell asleep and woke up, nothing changed.

It took nearly two days for him to realize that his life was in the dumps for real. He drifted from room to room, hearing echoes of the past. "Daddy, come say goodnight." "Honey are you coming up to bed?" First Jasmin's room, then Justin's, finally to his own—he kept seeing himself coming home and the excitement and laughter of those early years. Over and over in his mind he kept replaying what Crystal had said. At first he was angry, blaming her for everything. How could she be so ungrateful? He worked long hours so that he could provide her and the children with all the trappings of comfort and luxury. "I made sure Crystal didn't have to work!" his thoughts shouted. He thought, "The children went to private school, we live in a beautiful home, and this is what I get!"

He opened the liquor cabinet, retrieved a bottle of single malt he'd purchased from the duty free shop on a recent business trip to the UK, poured several fingers and added some ice from the bar fridge. He took a few sips while he browsed through his collection of music. Tilting his head, he focused on the titles: Elton John, Rod Stewart, Bob Dylan, John Lennon, Cat Stevens—each one held a story, every song brought back images—almost all of them involved Crystal. Jonathan's anger turned to self-pity, and the small sips of the whisky became large gulps.

Jonathan passed out in the middle of a song. Unaware, Rod Stewart sang on.

Six days passed in this way. On the seventh day, Jonathan's brother, Rob, came by with his wife, Sylvia. Time and time again they had phoned Jonathan's home, but no one answered and their messages were not returned. Worried, they called Crystal's mother and learned that Crystal had moved out. Now, they were even more concerned. Ringing the bell didn't wake Jonathan from his drunken slumber, so they resorted to banging on the door.

Finally, this worked.

Rob barely recognized Jonathan as he opened the door. Unshaven, untidy, with dark circles under his eyes, Jonathan greeted him perfunctorily in a thick voice, "What do you want?"

Rob and Sylvia tried to conceal their shock, and followed Jonathan into the house. Neither of them had seen him this way. Jonathan was always the successful and assured brother who had everything. The sight of him hung-over troubled and unsettled them both. Sylvia walked swiftly toward the kitchen to put on a pot of coffee. Rob gently steered Jonathan up the stairs, encouraging him to get cleaned up. Jonathan didn't argue. When he came back downstairs half an hour later, he was starting to resemble his old self.

Sylvia poured the coffee and Jonathan did the talking. He was obviously hurting. As he explained what had happened, he couldn't contain his tears. Rob and Sylvia had already had a long conversation with Crystal and knew the whole story, but they sat quietly and listened.

"For the first time in my life, I really don't see the need of going to work," Jonathan told them. "I'm questioning everything I believe. Is there any point to my life? And what am I going to do?"

Rob felt very concerned as he looked at the confusion and helplessness visible on his brother's face. He had never seen Jonathan in so much pain. What a difference a day makes he thought. One day you are at the top of the world seemingly in a perfect life. The next day, you have nothing. It made him want to examine his own life, but more than that he wanted to be there to help Jonathan through this.

"You can't keep doing what you've been doing over the last few days," Rob told him. "Closing out the world and trying to escape into a bottle doesn't help. Remember, you are still a father," he said sympathetically.

"I know the kids really miss you, and Crystal hasn't asked for a divorce," Sylvia said. "Maybe you can try and work things out."

Jonathan lifted his head. Noticing that Sylvia's words had touched Jonathan, Rob continued with a sincere tone. "Look, Bro, you need to get away for a while—you know, to clear your mind."

Jonathan nodded. "You're right. I need to do that. I can't think straight right now. But where would I go?"

It was ironic: over the last five years Jonathan had spent more time away than at home, yet he couldn't think of a single place to go. Just then, the doorbell rang. The newspaper boy had come to collect. Jonathan paid him what he owed, and in return, the newspaper boy placed seven days of newspapers into Jonathan's arms.

"I know! Take a look at the travel section, and find someplace interesting and different," Sylvia suggested.

Rob rummaged through the papers and pulled out the travel section. He opened it and the three of them moved their heads in tandem from left to right as they perused the ads. The advertisement on page three caught the attention of all of them at the same moment. Rob read aloud: "Experience of a lifetime—visit the Taj Mahal in exotic India." Rob looked at his brother with a loaded expression that said, Well?

Jonathan sighed, "Okay, I'll think about it."

The next day, Jonathan went back to work. As he

walked toward his office he noticed his colleagues were peering curiously at him.

"Nice to see you, Jonathan," his secretary, Wendy, said as he pulled out his black leather executive chair. As he sat down, she said, "Mr. Anderson left a message that he would like to see you as soon as you come in."

Russ Anderson was the president of the company. Since Jonathan had not been in to work for days, he thought he knew what the meeting was about. As he approached Anderson's office, Jonathan realized how out of place he felt. He really did not belong here.

"Well! Hello, Jonathan," Christine, Russ Anderson's personal secretary said. She seemed relieved to see him. "I'll let him know you are here." Moments later Christine spoke again, "He will see you now, and could I bring you a cup of coffee?" Jonathan nodded and entered the lion's den.

The drive to Brampton was relaxing, especially since, for a change, Jonathan did not have five places to get to in the same afternoon. But he felt a little apprehensive. He hadn't seen Crystal and the children in a week.

He switched from the tirade of insignificant news tidbits on the all-news station to some soft rock and immediately recognized the voice of Elton John singing "sorry seems to be the hardest word."

Jonathan turned down the volume as he reached the driveway. He sat for a moment, trying to compose himself, before getting out of the car. The walk to the door seemed like an eternity.

No sooner had Jonathan rung the doorbell than the door opened. Crystal stood before him, a breath of fresh air in a white dress and a violet apron. Her eyes spoke a welcome worth a thousand words. Jonathan was speechless, and his arms weighed a ton.

Crystal leaned forward in her usual manner to hug Jonathan, who tried without success to lift those arms and hold her tightly. As Crystal ushered him into the kitchen, he was assailed by the memory-evoking scent of a baking cake. Jonathan felt the sharp stab of a precious time now gone.

"The children are still at school, but they should be here soon," Crystal told him.

"I'm so looking forward to seeing them," Jonathan said, a catch in his voice.

Crystal and Jonathan talked for over an hour. It seemed like they had been apart for months, not days. Finally Jonathan told her that he had lost his job.

"How could they do this to you?" She was trembling in anger. "You've worked for them for ten years! The company could never have grown so much without the work you put in."

Crystal felt betrayed. She had seen Jonathan sacrifice everything for the company. Reaching out to touch Jonathan's hand she said, "You are strong, you are talented, and you are good at what you do. Finding something else won't be a problem for you." But finding something else was the furthest thing from Jonathan's mind. Nor did he see himself as particularly talented and strong at this point.

Just then, they heard the door open. "It must be the kids," Crystal said. "Mom was going to pick them up." As she opened the door, Justin shouted out, "Daddy's here!" He had seen the familiar car in the driveway. He ran to

11

Jonathan and presented him with his biggest hug. The events of the last few weeks had been particularly hard on Justin. Leaving home and his family surroundings was difficult enough, but Jasmin's accident had left him feeling very lonely and isolated. Justin's clinging did not go unnoticed as Jonathan reciprocated by planting some affectionate kisses on his cheek.

Expecting the same greeting from his daughter, Jonathan asked, "Where's Jasmin?"

Before Crystal could reply, Jasmin and her wheelchair entered the hallway. Jonathan ran to hug his little girl, who was flushed with excitement.

Jonathan stayed for supper and for a while it seemed that time had turned back. The children played and Crystal and Jonathan talked; it seemed no one wanted the evening to end.

Later, as Jonathan tucked the children into bed, Jasmin in particular was having a difficult time. "Are you Daddy's girl?" asked Jonathan.

"You know I am, Dad, but when can we all be together again?"

Jonathan looked away, pretending that there was something in his eye. "I'll be gone for a little while," he told her. "There are some things I need to do. But I'll come back, you'll see. Everything will be fine." He gave her a kiss, and then said, "Now you have to promise to take care of your mom. And don't get lazy about those exercises. I'm going to race you when I return."

She smiled then, and it made his heart glad.

Jonathan joined Crystal for a cup of coffee in the front room, and shared his thoughts about going away for a while, to think things through. Crystal felt very unsettled. She had hoped the separation would jolt Jonathan into re-examining his priorities. Deep inside she longed to work things out and hoped that Jonathan felt the same. Hearing that he wanted to go away wasn't what she had envisaged.

"Sure, if that's what you want to do," she said, choking back tears and trying to be supportive.

And then it was time to leave. Saying good-bye to Crystal was harder than anything he had done before, because deep inside he really did not want to leave, and there was no place else he wanted to go. As he gazed into her pretty face, he knew that he could not find fault in what she did. Crystal had not changed; she was still the same girl he married, always more concerned about living life simply with tenderness and passion.

I have built a wall around myself and have excluded all the things I cherished, he said to himself as he walked to the car. He wished desperately that things could be different.

Racing down the freeway, Jonathan was oblivious to the fact he was clocking 130 kilometres an hour. Bob Dylan was playing a concert at the Skydome tomorrow, the radio announced. Then a Dylan tune started playing and Jonathan turned up the volume. He knew every Dylan song, all of the words — they were the phantoms of his youth.

Dylan sang "Blowing in the Wind" and Jonathan's mind drifted. How far the world had progressed since those years of idealism. He recalled the times with Crystal, especially the university days, when they shared so many ideals. They had a purpose and conviction about the world, like that march in Washington to protest the

Vietnam War, that had cost them all their savings to get there. They stood for something; the idea of peace was a worthy cause. Yet how far have we really come and what have we learned since Dylan chided us for not listening to the "Pain of the Poor?"

He was so right, thought Jonathan. How many ears do we need to hear their cries. He recalled fondly how he had borrowed the money to get himself and Crystal to George Harrison's concert to aid the victims in Bangladesh. Bob Dylan had become a Pied Piper of sorts, inspiring our imagination and provoking our idealism. We had a sense of value for the people with whom we shared our planet. Whatever happened? he asked himself. The world had become a crowded island where friend and foe carried weapons of mass destruction. If ever the world needed hope, it was now.

Abruptly, the Dylan tune on the radio changed, jolting Jonathan out of his reverie.

It was "Like a Rolling Stone." Jonathan and Crystal knew every word to this song. They used to sing it together, enjoying cutting into the type of people in society they loathed: the superficial members of the establishment. They knew the price of everything and the value of nothing. They craved power and position and did not care how many people they deceived to get there. Material things mattered to them above everything, and they would crush anyone's spirit in order to win the prize they coveted. We would never become like them, Jonathan and Crystal had often boasted. The word "Napoleon" in the song triggered a reaction and Jonathan pulled over to the side of the road; he was gasping through streaming tears. Here, in the middle of nowhere, he could cry without being seen.

He had become everything he had loathed. Like Napoleon of Animal Farm, he had taken the very identity he despised. He had risen to the upper echelons of power, stepping on people along the way, and dismissing those who did not conform to the jungle culture of the business world. He had been ruthlessly ambitious. Bystanders became pawns as deceit and manipulation of the advertising business became an art form. He hobnobbed with politicians and movers and shakers, and, worst of all, he reveled in the power.

Jonathan had betrayed everything that had meant so much to him: his values, his ideals, and, yes, Crystal, too.

Slowly, Jonathan turned the rearview mirror to look at himself. He did not recognize the face that stared back at him. Wiping away his tears, Jonathan readjusted the mirror and, taking a deep breath, drove back onto the highway, ready to face the phantoms of his youth.

Meanwhile, Bob Dylan played on, and the sound of the harmonica seemed to cut through him like a knife.

Chapter 2

*"Tis certain that every seeker of Princedom
is thrown into captivity before he gains it."*[1]

Jonathan answered the door.

"Ready?" Rob asked.

"I'll just get my suitcase," Jonathan replied, and he bounded up the stairs. He felt as if the weight of the world had been taken off his shoulders.

Rob had offered to take Jonathan to the airport, while the trip to India was being hastily arranged. The ride to the airport was uneventful, and Rob pulled into the passenger loading zone sooner than Jonathan had expected.

"You don't have to wait," Jonathan told his brother. He was eager to get going. They said their good-byes and Jonathan headed to the check-in counter. He was booked on a two-week trip. The plan was to land in Bombay, then to tour for twelve days, then to finish in Delhi. The Taj Mahal was easily accessible from there.

The plane was on time and Jonathan, an experienced traveler, settled comfortably into his seat.

"Sir! Sir! Could you please fasten your seat belt?" The hostess woke Jonathan from a sound sleep while the plane was scudding through turbulence. For the next hour, the plane continued to be buffeted by strong winds. The passengers sat, glued to their seats. After what seemed a lifetime, an announcement from the captain finally came.

"We are having difficulties getting landing clearance in India. As a precaution, we have requested permission to reroute to Islamabad."

Jonathan seemed surprised; he was a seasoned traveler and had not encountered this before. "Just as well we are changing course, the weather will be calmer," said Jonathan to the nervous elderly woman sitting next to him.

Islamabad was in Pakistan. It was close to the Himalayan mountain range that separated the country from India.

The passengers left the plane at Islamabad airport and were provided coupons for a night's stay at the airport hotel. Jonathan checked into his room, freshened up and set out to explore the city in the early evening hours.

His first observation was that Islamabad was quite modern, used predominantly to house government offices and embassies. The taxi cost mere pennies, so he decided to ride beyond the main downtown center. Here, extreme poverty reigned. Jonathan sat in the cab and watched as thousands of city dwellers prepared to sleep on the side of the roads, on bridges and on the carts that some of them owned. Within the space of one hour, the city's landscape changed from a hubbub of commerce to a quiet gathering spot of the homeless.

Jonathan asked the driver to take him someplace where he could have a bite to eat. Only minutes later, the cabbie drew up in front of the Marriott Hotel.

"The patio outside is a good place, sir, and the food is good," the driver said.

Just as Jonathan reached into his pocket, the driver, not wishing to lose a fare, continued, "I will wait for you, sir."

Jonathan nodded, went in and asked to be seated on the patio. He was immediately escorted to a table outside, where the warm breeze was noticeable.

The menu was written in the local language. Jonathan attempted to decipher it but he did not have a clue what it said, and having built up an appetite, he was anxious to order. He turned to the table beside him and spoke to the man sitting there.

"Excuse me, but it looks like you can read the menu, and I could use some help."

"Sure I can," said the stranger. "Why not come join me at my table?"

"I am Jonathan," he introduced himself as he sat down across from the man.

The stranger reached out to shake his hand. "I am Dirum," he smiled. Just then, the waiter passed by. Dirum snapped his fingers and motioned him over. He said a few words, and in moments the waiter was back with another menu.

"Try this, it is in English. I think he gave you the wrong menu," Dirum said.

Jonathan was grateful. At least now he would know what there was to choose from. Before long Dirum and Jonathan were involved in conversation-the usual small talk. It was uncanny, but Jonathan felt at ease relating some of his problems that had led him to take this trip.

Dirum was a businessman from India; he too was only in Islamabad for one night.

"Where do you go tomorrow?" Jonathan asked him.

"I am taking a bus to Gilgit, higher up in the mountainous region. This time of the year, that's the only way

ANIL GIGA

to get there. What about you?" asked Dirum.

"Oh, me, I'm going to Bombay tomorrow. It's supposed to be an experience, I am told. I have certainly heard a lot about the Taj Mahal. Now, I am looking forward to seeing it," replied Jonathan. "But what will you do in Gilgit? Isn't it just a small town?"

"There is a guide in Gilgit; I am going to see him," Dirum answered. "Once in a while he takes people on a pilgrimage to meet a very enlightened man. It is now one of those rare occasions, and the timing is perfect for me. I guess we have something in common."

Jonathan looked puzzled. What can our destinations and lives have in common, he wondered.

Dirum answered his unasked question. "You left Canada because you hope that this journey somehow gives you the space to sort things out. You seek clarity about your own life, which is in a state of turmoil. I, too, am in this situation. There is more to life than just work-ing and raising a family. This place calls me, as it has you."

Jonathan was flabbergasted. For a moment, the two men stared at one another across the table. Dirum broke the silence. "Why don't you come with me? You will not find what you are looking for where you are going."

Jonathan sat up straight, and almost defensively he asked, "Why do you say that?"

Dirum looked thoughtfully into Jonathan's face before responding. "If you do not know where you are going, any road will take you there. The parts of India you are traveling to are tourist destinations; they are the Disneylands of Asia. Would you go to Disneyland to find space?"

Before Jonathan could answer, Dirum continued.

"Now, the Taj Mahal, that is a different story. But that place, when seen with the eye, has no value. You have bigger palaces in Vegas and Hollywood, that are cleaner and have more marble than the Taj Mahal."

"What do you mean?" said Jonathan, captivated with the conversation.

"The Taj Mahal is one of those rare places on earth, like the Grand Canyon, the pyramids, the Rockies, Stonehenge, Aswan — and there are others, some we know, some we do not. They are portals through which the energy of the universe flows strongly. If you are connected within yourself, you can go to these places and experience that energy."

"I am fascinated," Jonathan said. "Tell me more."

"Actually, there is another very compelling reason you may want to go with me," continued Dirum.

"And what is that?" Jonathan asked.

"The border between India and Pakistan was closed about two hours ago. India detonated a nuclear bomb that it has been developing. I guess any day now, Pakistan will respond with its own tests. There is a lot of military and political tension between these two countries. I do not think there will be any flights from here to India in the near future."

Jonathan could not believe what he was hearing. Panic started to seize him as he wondered, what now?

Dirum stood up. "I have to go now, get some rest. It will be a long journey. It was nice meeting you." With those words, Dirum left.

Jonathan watched as he walked away. For several minutes he sat and pondered the things Dirum had told him. When he stepped out from the front entrance of the Marriott, he found the taxi driver still waiting for him.

Back at his hotel, Jonathan soon learned that Dirum had related true events. The border was closed—in fact, that was the reason why the flight to India had been rerouted. The airline had given Jonathan few options: fly back to Toronto tomorrow, or wait and take your chances.

Jonathan thought about the three choices he had. Go back—which he really did not want to do. Stay in Islamabad until the border opens—which could take days or even weeks, and what would he do here? Finally, there was the allure of going on the pilgrimage with Dirum. Jonathan couldn't believe that he was seriously considering it—Dirum was a complete stranger who had offered to take him to a totally strange place.

He could be a criminal, for all I know, Jonathan told himself. Anyway, I don't know where he is or how to find him. I couldn't go even if I was sure I wanted to.

Jonathan concluded that his only option was to return home. Business experiences had taught him that when things are not going according to plan, you cut your losses. With this in mind, he repacked his suitcase for his journey back home the next day.

At six a.m., Jonathan was awakened by the haunting sound of a melodic voice coming from somewhere outside the window. It echoed through the streets from a turret at one of the mosques. It was a reminder to everyone in the vicinity that, for a moment, they should put aside their worldly activities and communicate with the higher power. Jonathan remembered, as a child, sitting with his mom and dad in church, singing "Oh Come, All Ye Faithful." The emotions evoked were similar; he felt at peace.

Just then, there was a gentle tap on the door. It was the bellboy. "A gentleman left this note for you," he said, and handed it to Jonathan.

To Jonathan's amazement, it was from Dirum. It simply read, "Meet me at the central bus station at 9 a.m., Dirum."

A nervous energy gripped Jonathan. Yes! He wanted to go! Glancing at his Rolex, he saw it was seven o'clock—enough time to get ready, have a hearty breakfast and get to the station.

The Islamabad bus station was unlike anything Jonathan had seen before. It did not come close to the orderly Greyhound stations back home. It was chaotic, with buses parked here, there, and everywhere, and people and porters intermingled, unloading and loading the buses as they came and went.

How on earth am I going to find Dirum here? Jonathan wondered. The sun was starting to heat up. Sweat began to run down Jonathan's face as he frantically looked in all directions. Just then, there was a tap on his shoulder.

"There you are," Dirum greeted him.

A relieved Jonathan hugged Dirum in his excitement and, before long, they were seated on the bus to Gilgit.

Dirum handed Jonathan a brown paper bag. Jonathan peeked inside. It was a roll of toilet paper! Before he could ask, Dirum smiled and said, "You will see."

The old bus bumped out of the station and rolled onto the thoroughfare. The ride was jarring, even to their teeth.

"This only lasts for two hours," said Dirum, a smile on his face. "After that, we will be traveling on the Karakoram highway through the Mountains. It will be a tough journey—twelve hours."

There was a long silence. Jonathan scanned the unfamiliar landscape. "You know, this is such a coincidence," he said.

"What do you mean?" asked Dirum.

"Well, the way I ended up in Islamabad, this war thing, how I met you and lost you, and now I am going with you to Gilgit."

Dirum did not respond immediately. He had a deep, thoughtful look. Then he turned to Jonathan and said, "There are no coincidences; everything happens for a reason."

Jonathan seemed perturbed by the answer. It sounded too mysterious and weird. But those words from Dirum consumed his thoughts for the next hour as he continued to look at the landscape out the window.

The bus veered off the local highway and headed into the mountains. Dirum was right, thought Jonathan, as the bus lurched over the bumpy road and negotiated the hairpin turns — this will be a rough ride.

Dirum interrupted Jonathan's thoughts, "Do you know why you are going with me?"

Jonathan nodded. "I think so. You know, when I was at university we often asked and discussed among ourselves those timeless questions like, who are we? What is our purpose? What is life? All those typical questions. After a while, as I moved on into a career and family, those questions just became clichés. Later still, I dared not to even think about them, for they affected my passion and drive. I guess I am at a point where I need some depth and meaning to my life."

"What do you mean, it would affect your passion and drive?" Dirum asked.

24

"Well, for example, when I was working on a very large cigarette company's account, our mandate was to structure an advertising theme that would increase the sales of cigarettes. Our performance in achieving sales targets determined whether we would retain the account the following year. If I were to have opposed certain advertising themes because it appealed to new smokers, many of whom were underage, I would have jeopardized the whole campaign. Losing accounts meant less profit and no bonuses. These are common situations. You stay focused on goals without any mental or emotional distractions."

"Oh," Dirum said, "you mean, like if a wolf worried whether the rabbit it was chasing had babies at home or something, then its pity might interfere with the hunt."

"Yes, like that," Jonathan replied.

A hint of sadness appeared on Dirum's face. "There is a difference between humans and animals," he said quietly.

Jonathan felt surprise at his own conclusions from that little discussion. As Dirum had pointed out, a lot of things he and others did may have been perfectly acceptable behavior in the animal world, but they were questionable ethical behavior by humans. With a guilty look on his face, Jonathan turned to Dirum and said, "Now you know why I need to meet that enlightened old man. I am confused about a lot of things; I need some answers."

"You and your microwave mentality," Dirum chided as his thoughts wandered. Too many people were innoculated from the pain and tragedies of the real world. Jonathan, like so many others, was oblivious to the daily struggle for survival by billions of people for whom living was not about life, death or finding meaning, but rather something very simple like the next meal.

"What do you mean?" asked Jonathan.

"You live in a world of instant gratification," Dirum said. He saw the puzzled expression on Jonathan's face and decided to continue, hoping his words wouldn't sound like an admonishment. "You want a home—it is easy for you. You make a call, set up the mortgage. If you need a car or furniture to dress up your home, you pick it up now and pay later. You need a woman, stop at the red light district. You want to gamble, you catch a plane for Las Vegas. You want to eat, phone and they will deliver. Instant gratification—that is how your society works. Everything in the world does not work like this. You want to go meet this wise man, get the answers instantly, then what? You live in a world of illusion because you come from a plastic society, where once you have all the comforts of life, you resign yourself to ask, 'what is the meaning of life?' If you want to know the meaning of life, just walk around the corner from your hotel room after dark! Experience the rush of fear at the sight of a million hungry eyes peering at you in the dead of night. Feel the pain of the women who put their crying babies to sleep with nothing more than hope for a better tomorrow. What is the meaning of life, is the wrong question. Instead ask, 'what is the meaning in my life?' This is where you will find the answers."

Jonathan thought these comments painted him as a lowlife, as someone superficial and ignorant. He searched within himself to find a defense but could not. That was the way he had lived his life and he could relate. The whole society was actually geared and structured to provide everyone instant happiness, Jonathan concluded.

It is plastic, an illusion. He could see that from his experiences in advertising. People buy things they do not need or cannot afford because we create the illusion that it will give them their cherished dream.

All those terrible-tasting cereals recorded huge sales increases, because we made women believe they would become slim. And those designer young-adult clothes at ridiculously high prices we promoted were grabbed up by young men who believed it would help them attract girls. My god, thought Jonathan, I have been living in Pinocchio's world. What is worse is that I have been as much the perpetrator as the victim. I, too, bought a Volvo because I believed it would keep Crystal and the kids safe in an accident. I bought a Rolex, not because it was a more accurate timepiece, but because I needed a status symbol. And now, thought Jonathan, like everyone else, I have been teaching these things to my kids!

Once again, Dirum interrupted Jonathan's thoughts. "The funny thing is, everyone else on this earth wants what you have. They risk their lives from as far away as Vietnam and China to enter into your illusion."

Jonathan once again drifted off into his own thoughts. It is an illusion, because people chase material things, possessions and status in the hope it will bring them lasting happiness. We mistake gratification for this happiness. The real picture tells the whole story, he thought. Society is under siege, with depression, poverty, violence, suicides. The family is under stress. Divorce is at an all-time high. Fragmentation and deep discontentment are painfully obvious. Look at Crystal and me, he thought, we both crave that illusive peace, yet the harder we have tried, the more pain we have felt.

Jonathan remembered his younger days with Crystal. Somehow the tone of this dialogue with Dirum gave a refreshing vitality in his thinking, something he had not felt since those youthful days when ideals were more important then status. He wanted to keep the conversation on the same subject, so he asked, "What about you, Dirum? Why are you going? You seem to have things figured out."

"There is a saying that, if all the trees in the world were pens and the oceans ink, then the ink would dry up before all the knowledge had been written," Dirum replied. "I am struggling. Some people struggle to get a big home or more wealth. I am struggling in my search for truth."

"The truth about what?" asked Jonathan.

"The truth about me, about my own essence," Dirum answered.

Jonathan changed the subject. "Well, how will meeting this enlightened man help? Do you have questions too?"

"No, I do not have questions," said Dirum patiently.

"I don't get this," Jonathan persisted. "What are you going to meet him for?"

Dirum looked at Jonathan pointedly. "Have you seen a bright full moon?" He asked. "Where does its light come from?"

"The sun," replied Jonathan, feeling like a child at school.

"Well," Dirum went on, "similarly, when in the presence of an enlightened soul, their energy radiates to other souls close by. In this country, we call it didar. By drawing that energy within us, the mirror of our own soul is cleansed. I think in the Western world, they call it the 'numinous experience.' It is nonrational. You could say that this creates an experience of the holy."

Dirum was about to continue, but he saw the blank look on Jonathan's face. "You won't understand," he said gently.

Jonathan pondered Dirum's words. They were piercing. He did not really understand. He was like a duck out of water, completely vulnerable. Yet the longer he thought about the things Dirum had said, the more they made sense.

Different people have different effects on me, Jonathan thought. When I was with my dad, I somehow always felt secure. There were some professors at the university whose company I craved because they made me feel so creative. Being in church as a child gave me the feeling of awe, as if I was in the presence of some higher being. Those were the positive energies I felt. Yet I despised being around some people—it made me feel so negative. It would make sense then, that if we were in the company of those spiritually elevated, we would feel their energy. This may explain why the disciples always wanted to be with Jesus, he thought. The idea of meeting the enlightened man in the mountains seemed comforting to Jonathan as he tried to fall asleep.

The Karakoram highway lived up to its reputation as one of the wickedest navigation nightmares anywhere. So narrow in some places that it was barely passable, the road scaled remarkable heights and meandered throughout the Himalayan mountain range. It wound through clouds. Frequent mudslides and avalanches added to both the difficulty and the danger of travel.

As Jonathan looked out the dusty window, he saw one of the rear wheels create a small rockslide as it struggled to hold onto the edge of the road. He was gripped by fear.

No one could survive an accident here, he thought, as he tried to see the bottom of the valley below the precipice on which they rode. These drivers must have fantastic concentration abilities to navigate these roads day and night at high speeds, he told himself, squeezing his eyes shut.

The bus was stopped. Dirum was saying something.

"Wake up, Jonathan, let us go outside to stretch." Dirum stood up stiffly. It had been four hours. Outside they saw a small village.

"Do you need to use a washroom?" Dirum asked.

Jonathan nodded urgently. "I'm dying to!"

"Follow me," said Dirum, briskly walking toward a grassy area at the edge of the village. "Find a spot anywhere here," he said when they reached the space. Jonathan stood still. He felt embarrassed.

"There are no toilets here, and none on the bus either," Dirum told him, amused. "Since the next stop isn't for another four hours, I suggest you forget your pride like everyone else." Noticing Jonathan had arrived without supplies, Dirum tossed him his roll of toilet paper and they both made a gracious attempt at giving each other privacy. They washed their hands with rainwater that had accumulated in a large drum barrel, then walked to the center of the village.

Inside a large oven pit in the ground, a man stood making fresh naan, the bread that was the staple food of the area. Jonathan and Dirum dug into a delicious hot naan and washed it down with a cup of tea made with milk. Then Jonathan took a short walk to the edge of the village and gazed out onto the mountain cliffs. It was an awe-inspiring sight. He would never have imagined that people actually lived here. The noise of breaking twigs caused him to turn around. It was Dirum.

"They call this place the roof of the world," he said quietly.

Jonathan responded, "As a child I used to stare at the clouds high up in the sky. Today I am walking in them; yet, why do I feel so insignificant?"

"Because you are," said Dirum, turning to walk back to the village. After a short distance, Dirum paused and said, "Then again, you are not."

What did he mean? Jonathan wondered, as he hurried to catch up with his friend.

The next four hours went by quickly. It was dark and most of the passengers, including Dirum and Jonathan, used the time to catnap. When they stopped again, all the passengers—men, women and children—rushed off the bus. The ritual of finding a spot to complete the washroom necessities seemed foremost on everybody's mind. When Jonathan returned to his seat Dirum was already there, almost asleep again. "Thank goodness for toilet paper," Jonathan remarked. "But I feel like an animal."

"You are," said Dirum in a sleepy voice, and few moments later, "then again you are not."

Jonathan felt slightly annoyed. "What's with all the riddles?" he asked. But Dirum was fast asleep. "That's smart. Now I'm talking to myself," Jonathan sighed. Then he, too, closed his eyes and soon drifted into sleep.

The bus rolled into Gilgit at around ten in the morning. Jonathan was surprised by what he saw.

"I can't believe you have a city this big way up here in the middle of the mountains," Jonathan commented.

Dirum was rubbing the sleep from his eyes. "The

Karakoram highway goes all the way from Islamabad in Pakistan to China," he said between a yawn and a stretch. "It is a major trading route and Gilgit is sort of in the middle, so it is an important location for all the traders."

Chapter 3

"Form is the shadow, reality is the sun.
The shadowless light is only to be found in the ruins."[1]

D irum and Jonathan unloaded their belongings and hailed a taxi. An old black car reminiscent of the '60s stopped to pick them up. "Where are we going?" Jonathan inquired as he shut the door.

"I have some friends — we will go there. They are expecting me," Dirum said.

"They won't mind me along?" Jonathan asked.

"No, I know them well," Dirum assured him.

Gilgit was a small city high up in the mountains, where the air was crisp and fresh. It had all the frantic activity of other Eastern cities, yet it had its own unique character. In addition to cars, there were carts pulled by horses and donkeys. Everyone, it seemed, had something to do. Even open streets were places of work. The sidewalk Jonathan observed was lined with kiosks and workshops that sold anything from snacks to trinkets. Meat from a cow or goat had been cut up and was being cured on the sidewalk.

The taxi stopped outside a modest-looking home. Jonathan and Dirum unloaded their suitcases and stood on the porch.

A man, perhaps in his fifties, appeared at the door and delightedly hugged Dirum while speaking rapidly in a language Jonathan did not recognize. Dirum pointed at him. The man rushed over and with equal enthusiasm hugged Jonathan.

He does not know me, Jonathan thought, I am a total stranger, yet he accepts me and offers me hospitality. Before long, Jonathan and Dirum were seated inside and were being served the traditional chai, the tea made with milk.

After Dirum and the man had got caught up with all the news, he turned to Jonathan and said, "We should go now and meet Mami."

"Who's Mami?" Jonathan asked.

"He is the guide I told you of. I have to ask him if you can join us on the pilgrimage."

"Do you think he might say no?" asked Jonathan worriedly.

"He can say no, but what I know of Mami, I don't think he will," and with those words Dirum stood to leave. Jonathan followed, still concerned that the whole trip might be wasted. Perhaps he will say no, Jonathan thought to himself. He was feeling very anxious. The idea of not having the opportunity to go on this pilgrimage to meet the enlightened man, when he so much looked forward to questioning him, troubled Jonathan.

"Don't look so nervous," Dirum said noticing the expression on Jonathan's face. "Everything happens for a reason—you have to learn to trust."

"But what if Mami says no?"

"Then that was what was supposed to happen," Dirum replied. "Instead of becoming disappointed, seek the lesson in every event. Learn from every experience. Remember, whoever has the power of reflection draws a lesson from everything. There is some good in all circumstances, no matter how disappointed we may be with an event."

It was a long walk through quiet streets. Jonathan wondered to himself how Mami would respond. Forty minutes later, at the edge of the suburb, he saw a small cottage. A vegetable garden at the rear was filled with tomatoes.

"Wait here," Dirum said as he knocked on the door. An ancient-looking woman opened the door. A few words were exchanged and she disappeared into the house. Soon she returned and more words were spoken. Dirum turned to the nervous Jonathan and motioned him to come to the door. "You can go inside," Dirum said.

Feeling rather relieved, Jonathan entered and was shown to a room where some chairs stood empty.

A few moments later, the old woman returned. To Jonathan's surprise, she spoke to him in English: "Mami would like to know who you are."

"My name is Jonathan Tsol," he said. "I am from Canada."

The old lady disappeared and returned moments later.

"Mami would like to know who you are," she said again, this time very slowly and precisely.

Jonathan thought: I probably didn't give him enough information about myself. Mami will be impressed with my credentials.

"I have a degree in economics and an MBA from Harvard," he told the woman. "I have sat on the corporate boards of three large public companies. In addition, I have been appointed to the arts council and the advisory board of the Red Cross. I am forty-four years old, married with two children," he said rather proudly.

Once again the old lady went away and then, moments later, reappeared. "Mami says that all the things you mentioned have been acquired by you. He asks again, who are you?"

Jonathan was confused. He didn't know how to answer this question. It was the simplest question, yet he had no answer.

Mami is right, Jonathan thought. My wife, my children, my education, even my own name, I have simply acquired. So who am I? In an age when we have space missions to Mars and the quantity of knowledge doubles every month, what little we know about ourselves. We simply cling to those things we have acquired.

"Precisely!" exclaimed a voice from the hallway.

Jonathan looked up and saw a sixty-something gentlemanly figure in a caftan gown walking toward him.

"We have taken the things we have acquired and made them masks behind which we hide," the man said. "The mask is security, and man is afraid to remove it. When we have the mask we can project images of status, of calmness and command. Yet remove the mask, and what are we?"

The words stopped and the gentlemanly figure stood before Jonathan. "Nice to meet you, Jonathan. I am Mami and I am sorry I kept you waiting," he said as he stretched out his hand.

Jonathan responded by shaking his hand firmly, utterly amazed at how Mami had not only captured his very thought, but also had provided the missing conclusion he was struggling with.

"So, you wish to journey with us to meet Ila, the enlightened one," he said.

"I would be very thankful," answered Jonathan nervously.

"It is a long trip; there are many days of walking. It can be difficult." Mami peered into Jonathan's face.

The words unsettled Jonathan. He had no idea that meeting the wise old man would involve a trek through mountainous terrain on foot. After a moment's consideration, he said, "I really wish to meet the enlightened one, I have many questions."

Mami smiled. "Very well then, you may join us. We shall leave tomorrow."

When Jonathan emerged from the cottage, Dirum was waiting outside. "Well?" he asked loudly.

Jonathan smiled and Dirum returned the smile before continuing, "I told you to trust, did I not?"

Jonathan remained quiet, still mesmerized by the meeting with Mami. Then he said, "He reached deep within me and touched something. With just his thoughts and presence he gave me an awareness of my own being."

Dirum remained silent, obviously not wanting to break Jonathan's spell.

"We create illusionary images behind which we exist," Jonathan continued. "It is a prison. The very thing that enables us to command has become a jail in which we are confined. Dirum, I don't even know who I am. I have worn this mask for so long that I have forgotten my true essence," he said passionately.

Seeing that Jonathan was in a very agitated emotional mood, Dirum refrained from speaking. After a time, he realized that Jonathan needed a catalyst to help him understand.

"I met a Wise-man once, who told me that our condition is like that of a bird in a cage," Dirum said. "After a long time of imprisonment the bird has forgotten that it can fly; it no longer even has a memory of it. When the bird is given the opportunity to fly away from the cage, it will resist, because it no longer understands the concepts of freedom. Furthermore, it fears to fly, as it has no confidence. The situation of man, the Wise-man told me, is similar. We have forgotten our true origin, and, like the bird, we feel secure in our prison. When man truly comes to realization, he will recite these words: 'A bird I am, the body was my cage, but I have flown, leaving it as a token.'"

The two men walked for a while and Jonathan spoke again, "How can you tell when someone is enlightened and wise?"

"Enlightened souls emanate spiritual energy, just as petals of a flower emanate a fragrance," answered Dirum.

Then Mami is enlightened, thought Jonathan to himself.

Noticing Jonathan was struggling with himself, Dirum put his arm around his shoulder and said, "There is something enduring and noble in all of us. The question — Who am I? — leads to the discovery of something within us which is beyond the mind and is infinite. If we never ask this question we are like an elephant, which in its life will walk enough miles to go around the world twice, wandering hopelessly. It is only when we ask, who am I, that our quest begins. That is when our life starts, for it is the point when we finally have the courage to remove our masks."

Jonathan looked almost dejected. "You are right; it is this quest that enables us to emerge from the illusion. I am forty-four and my life has just begun," Jonathan admitted.

It could be worse, he thought, trying to put a positive spin on the realization. Some people never, ever, remove their masks. They die in the illusionary world!

Later that afternoon, Dirum seemed preoccupied in socializing with the family of their hosts, so Jonathan decided to wander around the quiet neighborhood. He missed Crystal and the children. As he neared some stores and kiosks, he began to look for gifts he could purchase for them.

The choice for Crystal was easy, since many stores had beautiful hand-woven miniature blankets, called shoals. She would love one of these, thought Jonathan, rummaging through the selection. Further along the street he found a handcrafted spinning top for Justin.

Finding something for Jasmin was proving to be a dilemma. Then he came across an old-looking store. The sign read, Rabbya Store. It seemed to have everything, similar to the Dollar Plus stores in Toronto, except it was a dark store and most of the items were old and second-hand.

After a while, an old woman appeared. "Can I help you?" she asked in a friendly voice.

"I am looking for a gift for my daughter. She is seven. I am searching for something really special."

The look on the woman's face changed and she spoke in a stern, motherly way. "Why don't you stop drinking and spend more time with her? Give her your time and attention, that would be the best gift."

Jonathan was taken aback. His first reaction was to walk out. What happened to "The customer is always right," he thought. If she doesn't want my business, I will go elsewhere. But then his mind flashed back to what Dirum had said on the bus: "Many enlightened souls walk among us. Listen and you will teach yourself. Consider not who speaks, but what is said." One sentence in particular came back again and again. "If you become receptive, what you need to do or hear will find you."

Jonathan looked at the old lady. "I don't understand," he said. "I have stopped drinking."

The woman smiled. "Alcohol is not the only thing that can intoxicate us."

Jonathan stared at her blankly.

"Do not be so intoxicated by the things of the material world," she continued. "The greatest of all treasures is the everlasting nobility of your soul. What your daughter needs is not things, but your time. She needs to feel your love."

Jonathan pictured Jasmin in the wheelchair and knew that one hug, one kiss, just one moment holding her would be worth far more than any gift that would be forgotten the next day. The world does intoxicate us, he thought. Whether it is wealth, possessions or status, we are consumed by them. Surely there is a life beyond consumerism. We seek happiness for ourselves and others as if it were a product. We mistakenly believe that if we work hard enough, if we strive enough and plan it, happiness is ours.

The old lady interrupted Jonathan's thoughts. "There are a lot of valuable things in this old store," she said, and left to attend to her work.

As Jonathan wandered around the store, engrossed in his thoughts, he tinkered with the variety of old and used items. A box of old cassettes caught Jonathan's eye and he began to flip through the titles. He was amazed—they must have been made over twenty years ago. The Who, Led Zeppelin, the Faces, Peter Frampton, John Mayal and the Cream—all familiar bands from the '70s and '80s. Jonathan picked up the final cassette and blew the dust off. It was a Supertramp cassette called Breakfast in America. He was immediately flooded with memories.

It was 1982. Jonathan sat by the window in his apartment with a pair of headphones covering his ears. Crystal came in and Jonathan stood up, removed the headphones and gave her an affectionate hug, followed by a kiss. "So I'm in class all day and you're lounging around at home," she teased him.

"I got lucky, I didn't have any classes today," Jonathan responded.

"So what did you do?" Crystal asked.

"Oh, I slept in a little, then I picked up the latest Supertramp album. It is really good! Listen to this track — it's my favorite, it's called the Logical Song." He put the headphones on Crystal. The song played.

Throughout the song Jonathan's thoughts identified with the words. Our purity and innocence is lost soon after birth. As life takes over and molds us, we lose our own identity. But at some point in our life we have to ask the question, who am I?

The song ended and Jonathan's thoughts returned to the present. Somehow he had given up on the quest he had back then; now he had a second chance.

Jonathan picked up the cassette and gave it to the woman of the shop. "You are right, there are many valuable things here," he said.

"So this cassette is for your daughter?" she queried.

"No, the cassette is for me. I am planning to give my daughter something more precious," Jonathan responded.

The old lady smiled again, and, touching Jonathan's hand in a maternal way, she said, "Then let me tell you a story before you go."

"There was a man who wished to find happiness. Because of his goodness, he was taken to paradise for one day. He felt very happy. There was a market, and he was informed that in the market he could get any dream. So the man, feeling very thankful about the opportunity, went and asked for all the things that he cherished, that would bring him happiness on earth.

"'I wish my children to be happy and righteous, I wish prosperity, I wish unity and love with my wife, I want peace on earth, oh, and I want happiness and success for everyone,' he said.

"The face in the stall looked at the man and said, 'Sorry, but we don't sell fruit, only seeds.'"

The old lady finished this story by saying, "May you be blessed in your pilgrimage."

Jonathan thanked her and headed back to the house. One thought preoccupied him: what did she mean by "we only sell seeds" and how did she know that I was going on the pilgrimage?

He turned the corner and started to hurry. The old lady was trying to tell me something, he thought.

When he reached the house, Dirum seemed quite relieved to see him. "Oh there you are," he said. "We have to leave early in the morning, and I have got you a backpack. You might as well leave the rest of your belongings here."

Jonathan thanked him as he took his backpack and went into the room to pack. It was a small pack and by the time he had stuffed in the items Dirum had put aside for him—like the blanket, sleeping bag, water bottle, an old winter jacket and gloves—there was little room left. Jonathan added a few of his own clothes and zipped up the pack. No sense in taking credit cards, traveler's checks, passports and shaving things, he thought. Pulling out his fanny pack, Jonathan put in his local currency rupees, some gum and a photograph of Crystal and the children.

When Dirum came into the room to pack, Jonathan was already in his bed.

"You seem distracted," Dirum said.

"I'm just a little anxious," Jonathan answered. "A lot has happened since I met you. There was a time when I was so sure about everything, so self-confident, but since I met Mami, I am not so sure about anything."

"Do you regret anything?" Dirum asked.

"I guess I see this as a second opportunity to do the things I should have done a long time ago," Jonathan responded in a reflective tone.

"You cannot live your life looking backwards," Dirum said. "Regrets become baggage that stifles your journey. Each new day is the beginning of the rest of your life — you can choose to live it differently."

Dirum jumped into his own bed, flicked the light switch, and then began reciting a poem by the Persian poet, Omar Khayyam.[2]

The moving finger writes and, having written, moves on.
Nor all your piety or wit shall lure it back to cancel half a line,
Nor all your tears wash out a word of it.

Chapter 4

"This world, indeed is the poison of your souls:
oh, go in yonder direction, for there lies your open sky."[1]

Jonathan was the first to awake in the morning. The thoughts of meeting Ila, the enlightened one, had kept him tossing and turning late into the night.

After a breakfast of chai and bread, Dirum and Jonathan set off to meet up with Mami. When they reached his cottage, they could see a group of four people in the yard. As they got closer, they recognized the old woman of the house as one of them, but the three men were unfamiliar.

When they joined the group, the woman greeted them. "These three men will be accompanying you," she told them.

They introduced themselves as Arjun, Raj and Gulam. At first Jonathan had a problem pronouncing the names, but it did not take him long to get a conversation going, and soon he was able to put the right name to each face.

Two old Jeeps pulled up and at that point Mami emerged from the cottage, wearing a light caftan gown. He had put on a turban to protect his head from the heat of the sun.

As the Jeeps pulled away, Jonathan's baseball cap made for a noticeable contrast to his companions' headgear. The Jeeps drove into the Hunza district, through a number of small towns and communities. The roads were rough and the terrain was difficult. Their four-wheel-drive vehicles were ideally suited to the task.

After about four hours of driving, the cars came to a halt at the end of the road. The five companions unloaded their gear while Mami had a short chat with the drivers that sounded like a long thank-you.

"Now we walk," said Mami, as he picked up his staff and began heading into the foothills of the Himalayas. It reminded Jonathan of those images he had seen as a kid of the biblical Abraham and his staff. It seemed surreal.

As far as the eye could see, the foothills seemed barren. The forestation had been cut for lumber or cleared for agricultural land. Very little wildlife was noticeable. With their habitat destroyed, most species of wild goat, tiger, rhinoceros, musk deer, wolf and snow leopard were restricted to protected areas, such as the Kaziranga sanctuaries, although occasionally they did venture out.

On the way, Dirum gave a history lesson.

"Himalaya came from a Sanskrit word, which meant 'abode of snow,'" he told Jonathan. "This was earth's highest mountain range, containing nine of the ten highest mountain peaks in the world. The highest was Mount Everest, at 29,028 feet. K2 was the second highest at 28,251 feet."

Jonathan recalled seeing K2 from the bus on the way to Gilgit.

"The mountain system developed 35 million years ago, with powerful earth movements," Dirum continued. "The Himalayas were formerly deposits in the ancient sea, which were raised up. The region is in a continual state of flux. Earthquakes and tremors are frequent."

There were no more towns ahead, just barren land, and the harsh weather and terrain made it very difficult to have a transport system. Still, people survived. The poverty was noticeable, and small clustered settlements were spread out, especially in the high valleys.

After the first few days traveling, the weather change was noticeable and everyone put on their winter coats, hats and gloves, especially after the sun set.

During the early evening, they set up camp. Mami had indicated where and when. A fire was lit and everyone sat around it.

"It is cold," Jonathan remarked to the group.

Suddenly everyone burst out laughing. Then Raj said, "This is summer. Sometimes we have to travel in the winter; now that is cold!"

We have it so good, thought Jonathan. It gets cold in Canada, but how often do people travel outside in the cold for any length of time? Buses, cars, trains and shelters all combine to shield people from the cold. With no electricity, even the small cement dwellings we saw on the way must feel like refrigerators, he mused.

Very soon, everyone was tucked into their sleeping bags around the fire. Conversations were short that night, and the noise of snores echoed in the darkness, competing with the fireflies, frogs and owls.

Jonathan was not used to sleeping on the ground, and furthermore, the cold chill made him very uncomfortable. He awoke early, thinking he was the first one up. As he glanced around, to his surprise, he saw Mami sitting on a rock in the lotus position, meditating.

Dirum interrupted Jonathan's observation of Mami. "Good morning. You slept okay?" he asked.

"I am not used to this," Jonathan said in a complaining voice. "I like a warm bed in a warm house; a hot shower in the morning is a must; then, of course, that first cup of coffee."

"Do you realize that only ten percent of the world's population has that?" Dirum responded.

Ten percent, thought Jonathan, means there are some five-and-a-half billion people who would consider that a luxury.

"In this region," Dirum continued, "life is tough. The women have to walk sometimes up to ten miles each day just to fetch clean water. The death rate among children is very high. One hundred and ninety-four out of every thousand children will die by the time they are five years old from preventable diseases. There are no hospitals or schools, and the men work long hours just for subsistence."

"What about aid from the Western world?" Jonathan asked sympathetically.

"Not much of it gets to these remote regions. There are some private philanthropic foundations that collaborate with international development agencies. They make a difference, but so much more remains to be done."

Looking around, Jonathan noticed that Mami was still in rapt meditation. "What does he think about in meditation?"

"Meditation is not about thinking, it is about feeling the energy of the universal soul," Dirum answered, as he started to roll his sleeping bag. Jonathan almost asked what he meant by the universal soul, but he held back, noticing Dirum in the midst of packing.

The next five hours of walking took its toll on the group. It was tiring, especially during the day when the sun drained everyone's energy.

For Jonathan, Mami was a source of great inspiration. He said little but, whenever he did, his words were loaded with wisdom. Jonathan made great efforts to listen intently whenever Mami spoke. Like an eager student, he felt like a child in Mami's presence. All along, the image of him sitting in meditation was vividly ingrained in Jonathan's mind.

By the end of the second day, the weariness among the group was evident. Jonathan had replaced his baseball cap with a turban because it protected his neck and ears from the heat of the sun. "I look like Lawrence of Arabia," Jonathan said to himself.

The second day's camp was set up by a small lake. The water was crystal-clear, and throughout the evening women from nearby settlements came to collect it. Jonathan had a better night only because he was too tired to notice the discomfort.

The first thing Jonathan noticed as he awoke in the morning was Mami in meditation, silhouetted against the sun. This was an image that continued to captivate his imagination from that day forward.

After two days spent traveling, the lake offered a great opportunity to bathe and freshen up.

"It's cold!" said Jonathan as his feet touched the water.

"Just dive in. It is the only way," Dirum called, who was already splashing around in the lake.

Jonathan complied, diving in headfirst, and emerging a short distance from Dirum. "This feels good," he said.

Soon Arjun, Raj and Gulam joined them. As Jonathan took another dive into the water, he felt his Rolex slip off his wrist. He resurfaced in a state of panic.

"My Rolex! My Rolex!" he shouted. "I've dropped it in the water!" Gulam and Arjun, who were the closest, stared at Jonathan, trying to understand what he was saying. They were not familiar with the word.

Dirum swam over. "It is his watch, he has dropped it in the water." Everyone joined in frantically searching the water. Jonathan was in a frenzy as he looked underwater, holding his breath for as long as he could.

In the meantime, Mami sat silently, no longer meditating but observing the panic-stricken activities of the group. "Come," he called, motioning the group to leave the water. Jonathan did not want to, but Dirum called to him, "Let's go."

Mami invited everyone to come sit beside him.

"Allow the water to be still and it will reveal to you that which you seek," he said in an assured voice. The group sat for about twenty minutes. During this time the movement of the water became still once again and all the silt from the lake's floor resettled at the bottom. Mami looked at Jonathan and said, "Go retrieve your watch."

With some apprehension, Jonathan waded into the calm, clear waters of the lake. The bottom was easy to see. Glancing around, he noticed the shiny golden object and reached to pick up his watch. He emerged like a student who had learnt something about life. "Thank-you very much," said Jonathan sincerely. He returned to the group, thinking that Mami seemed so above the situation.

Just then, Mami looked at Jonathan and said, "The water is like life. Approach it in the same way and it, too, will reveal what you seek."

Later, Jonathan sat alone contemplating those words. A picture of Mami meditating kept reappearing in his mind. Mami was right, Jonathan thought, because we approach life as if it were an emergency, and then we respond with panic or fear. Sometimes, we worry, or become anxious—we "sweat the small stuff," muddying the water and making things worse. Life is like the water: the more we approach it with stress-filled responses, the more confused things become. We have to respond calmly, by silencing our minds, which is the perpetrator of fears.

About two hours after they had set off on their third day's journey, they stopped at a small settlement. Such settlements were common along the way. The settlers were always friendly, willing to extend their hospitality at every opportunity. These were important pit stops where the companions were able to rest and get fed.

"Look," Dirum exclaimed, pointing to some construction taking place in the distance. "There is an example of the type of aid project you see once in a while."

A large sign in green identified the project's sponsors. It read, "This project is a collaboration between the AKDN and the Canadian International Development Agency."

Jonathan seemed visibly proud. He pointed at one of the supervisors. "Ask him about the project," he said to Dirum.

Dirum walked across and chatted with the supervisor for a while, then returned to where Jonathan stood. "These agencies do not work like the Red Cross, which is a relief organization providing temporary help," said Dirum. "You cannot help the people in these remote areas by helping today and not being here later. This creates a dependency, making it a bigger problem in the end. The philosophy of the AKDN, which is a private, nongovernmental, philanthropic foundation, is simple: feed a man a fish today and you have to feed him again tomorrow; teach him how to fish and he feeds himself for the rest of his life."

Jonathan was fascinated. "It is so true. Relief organizations like the Red Cross play an important role during disasters and other urgent situations. In the long term, however, you need a different approach. How come this method is not used in Africa and other regions of the world where poverty is also prevalent?"

"If you ask me, the wealthier nations don't do enough to begin with," said Dirum, disappointment in his voice.

As the companions left the settlement to resume their journey, they were met by another small group of four going toward the enclave they had just left behind. After the usual greetings, Raj and Arjun seemed to be engaged in a long discussion with the other travelers.

"What are they saying?" Jonathan questioned Dirum, who was listening intently.

"The travelers are coming from the same place where we are going. They say that if we turn right ahead, we can save a whole day of traveling."

This tweaked Jonathan's interest. This was the third day. If they could save a whole day of traveling, then they could be there within another day. The thoughts of meeting Ila, the enlightened one, had kept Jonathan focused, but the days were hard, wearing him down. "That sounds really great," Jonathan said.

The travelers said good-bye and continued past the companions. Raj and Arjun were now involved in a deep discussion with Mami.

"What is happening now?" Jonathan asked.

"Well Raj and Arjun want to take the shortcut," Dirum replied. "They said these travelers just came from there and it would save them a lot of time. However, Mami does not want to."

"Why not, if it is a shorter, faster route to our destination?" Jonathan asked, hoping to avoid an extra twelve hours on foot.

Just then, Mami approached Dirum, Jonathan and Gulam and calmly said, "Raj and Arjun wish to take the shortcut the travelers spoke of. It is a faster route, but there are risks on that path. I shall be traveling in my planned direction; you can accompany me or you are free to go with Raj and Arjun."

Jonathan's first instinct was to follow Raj and Arjun. That was the quickest way; however, the idea of leaving Mami troubled him. Dirum turned to Jonathan and asked, "Well, what do you want to do?"

Jonathan thought deeply and said, "I trust Mami's path."

Dirum smiled. "I do too," he agreed. Then they turned and looked to Gulam for his decision.

Gulam was a quiet fellow; he rarely had anything to say. Those times that he did speak, he was merely inquiring about things. It was rare for him to take much interest in any discussion. He seemed just happy to tag along with Mami.

In the end, Raj and Arjun took the shortcut while Dirum, Jonathan and Gulam followed Mami.

That evening, the gathering around the fireplace was both smaller and quieter. The thought of where Arjun and Raj were, and how they were doing, preoccupied Jonathan.

In the distance a dog wandered into the meadow. As he busied himself marking his territory, another dog appeared. They sniffed one another according to their ritual, and before long the larger dog mounted the smaller female one. Their copulation was swift, and both of them immediately wandered off again in different directions.

Jonathan and Dirum had watched the entire scenario, and, after its conclusion, Dirum turned to Jonathan and said, "Do you remember what you said on the bus about animals?"

Jonathan thought about it briefly. "Yes I do. I said I felt like an animal and you had said, 'You are, and then again you are not.'"

"Well let me explain. Human beings have a higher and a lower self. The lower self acts from our animalistic instincts, while the higher self acts from the energy of the universal soul. Man alone has a choice. Nafs-a-mutmaina identifies the higher self in man. Nafs-a-amara is identified with the lower self. The dog we saw will act as a dog. Its habits and actions are mostly predictable. The human, however, can debase himself and act as an animal or raise himself up and act nobly. Every act a human engages in emanates from the higher or lower self. Man alone has a choice," Dirum said, answering the question Jonathan had posed earlier.

Jonathan reflected upon it for a time. All the wars and conflicts that take place in our world — in essence, these are territorial conflicts, and that is how animals behave. The irony was that these were the attributes of the people we choose to lead our nations. If they choose to act from the lower self, then it is no surprise to see aggression and struggle for domination. Yet Jonathan also saw the expressions of the lower self in the corporate world he came from. How different the world would be if the leaders we chose operated from their higher self, he thought. It is true; a lot of things we do are primeval. Yet we also have the choice to rise up and be more. The crackling of the firewood interrupted Jonathan's solemn mood. "Tell me more of this," he said, engrossed in the subject.

Dirum was at a loss for words; the discussion was entering a realm that was beyond his ability to articulate. He looked up to Mami in the hope that he would satisfy Jonathan's thirst for answers. Jonathan, sensing this, turned to look at Mami, too. He felt a sincere and tender bond with him and valued his words.

"Creation has a duality, that which is perceptible and that which is imperceptible," Mami said. "The perceptible is the physical creation. The imperceptible is the spiritual. Natural laws exist within both these realms."

Mami paused, allowing Jonathan to absorb what he was saying, and then he continued. "We have come to understand well the laws in our perceptible world, that is our physical world. The law of gravity, the law of aerodynamics, of inertia—these are examples of physical laws. Because we understand them we align our lives accordingly. People will not ordinarily jump from a high building, because we understand that fighting the law of gravity can only harm us. In the old days, people tried to fly. They made all sorts of contraptions and machines with which they jumped off the cliffs in the vain hope of soaring. They were not stupid; they just did not understand the laws of aerodynamics. Once man was able to understand these laws, engineering a plane that could fly became easier. We understand physical laws and act in ways that avoid the clash, for the laws of physics will ultimately prevail."

Jonathan jumped in enthusiastically, "We have made it into a science. We learn of these laws from the time we are born, and we survive because of them."

"That's right," Mami said, "whether it's heat, cold, fire or water, whether it's the human body or any created thing-everything in the physical realm conforms to a physical law."

Jonathan was mesmerized by his thinking and looked up to Mami and said, "Go on, tell me more."

Mami continued, "Similarly there is the imperceptible world. Some call this the spiritual realm, and there are spiritual laws that exist, and everything conforms to them. Yet man only understands them in a minute way."

Jonathan interjected, "So you have creation, which has a physical and spiritual realm. How do we humans fit into this picture?"

Mami answered, "There is a perfect order within creation. From the lowest plant life to trees, from the lowest animal life to humans, from the cycles of rain and the tides, the orbits of the sun and the moon, there is a perfect balance. But in addition there is a hierarchy, and right at the top of this chain of creation is the human. He is the highest within the created world. We call him the ashraful maklukat."

"What does it mean?" Jonathan inquired.

"The highest created being," Dirum said, who was learning as much from this as was Jonathan.

Mami continued, "The human being is unique within creation. We have been endowed with the faculties of the perceptible world and the imperceptible world. We are, in other words, physical and spiritual. Our physical self is perceptible and lives within the laws of this physical world and in this state we are no different than the cow, the goat, the lion, and even a tree. In fact, at this material level, we are made up of the same recycled elements as the tree or dog, that being carbon, hydrogen, oxygen, nitrogen, and so on. It is said that a cow is worth more dead than we are, because its leather at least has value, like its meat. However, our spiritual self is imperceptible and conforms to spiritual laws."

"Tell me more about our spiritual self," persisted Jonathan. He craved a better understanding of the mystical.

Mami obliged. "The essence of our spiritual self is the soul, although different people have somewhat different terminologies. It can be referred to as the spirit, the soul, the athma, but these are just semantics."

"What is it made of? Where does it come from?" Jonathan interrupted.

Mami took a breath and continued. "In the same way our physical bodies are made of the same substance as the physical world, our spiritual essence is made up of the same substance as the universal soul which sustains creation. As we can draw on the energy of the physical realm, we can do the same with the spiritual. We can draw its energy. This is what makes us unique and separates us from the animals."

Again, Jonathan interrupted. "What kind of energy do you mean?"

Mami eased back into his explanation. "Man can tap into the energy of the material world and find physical prosperity — whether it is the precious metals we mine, the chemicals we create, the medicine we produce to make our lives more comfortable, the technology we use to travel and to build. These are all aspects of prosperity we get from the physical realm. Animals cannot do the same. How does a lion cure a broken leg? How does a bird mend its broken wing? How does a goat shelter itself from a flood? Truly we are endowed with gifts that can enable us to prosper. We only progressed from primitivity when we learned to master these physical laws. Similarly, we are also endowed to tap into the prosperity of the spiritual realm. However, in most cases, man is so enamored with the prosperity of the physical world that he often neglects the spiritual. The results are often devastating and tragic."

Now Dirum interjected, "What do you mean?"

Mami paused to stoke the fire, and then continued. "Man is a physical and spiritual being, and both aspects need to be nourished to reach the harmonious level of existence. If we were to be preoccupied existing on just one level of being, then the harmony would be broken. After all, it is akin to traveling in a plane with two propellers when only one is functioning. For a time, the engine will carry the load, but after awhile, the consequences and impact will be felt. In the same way, if we function only on the physical level, attached and gratified purely by physical and material things, then the consequences will emerge. The barbaric manners of murderers and rapists may be extreme examples of a human body devoid of a soul, but depression, sadness, discontentment and unhappiness are common ailments of the increasing detachment from our spiritual selves. Suicide, violence and anger are often consequences of the confused state of being. It is ironic, but tapping into the prosperity of the spiritual realm is really the missing piece. If only they knew it is the more important."

"Why?" asked Dirum.

Throwing yet another log on the fire and clasping his hands over the warmth, Mami continued. "The physical and material realm with which we are so familiar is temporal and finite. It is limited in space and time. Our physical aspects, our bodies, are also subject to the laws of this realm. We age and our bodies decay, as does everything else. So all that we have is temporary.

"The spiritual realm, on the other hand, is infinite and eternal. It has dominion over all physical things because it existed before physical creation and will exist long after. However, the most important aspect is that the soul in man is made of the same substance as the universal soul, which sustains both realms within creation."

"So," said Jonathan, trying to understand precisely, "the soul or spirit within each human is made of the same substance as that of the universal soul which sustains the creations at all times?"

"Exactly," Mami replied. "Look at this fire. If the fire is the universal soul, than these sparks of fire that emanate from it are the souls. The closer the souls are to the fire, the brighter they glow." Mami tossed on another log, creating a flurry of sparks.

"I understand!" Jonathan exclaimed. "It is so clear! I mean, now that I think of it, it makes so much sense. The closer we are to the universal soul the more illuminated we became, and the more enlightened we are, the greater is the experience of meaningful happiness. Yet why is this idea of spirituality still very much an enigma?"

The warm glow of the fire in the darkness reflected on Mami's face as he responded. "It is hard to see the darkness in the bright glow of the sun, similarly can we feel the air inside the depth of the ocean?" he asked.

Dirum, Jonathan and Gulam shook their heads to answer, no.

"Then how can we feel the existence and the reality of the spiritual realm while we are fully intoxicated in the material one?" Mami asked rhetorically. "The very tools of science and rational thought that enabled us to understand our physical environment and make so much progress in it are turned towards the understanding of the spiritual environment. Yet these are blunt and useless instruments in this endeavor."

"How can we, for example, turn to scientific research to learn about our own spirituality? How can worldly knowledge, which negates the existence of the soul, help us in knowing our true essence? It forces us to live an exoteric existence totally ambivalent to our esoteric essence. The consequence," Mami continued with some passion, "is that those sharp points of distinction between the physical and spiritual have become blurred, the real nature of man's essence has become hazy, and we have instead the emergence of the techno-human being."

Jonathan was deeply touched, for he saw in himself the very symbol of the dilution, deviation, distortion and delusion that had led to this plight within society. "Is there anything we can do?" he asked.

"As a society, we have to engage in the rediscovery of our true nature," Mami replied. "We cannot use the tools of rational thought, nor of science. Instead, we must look at ourselves as a part of creation, rather than a separate entity. In the process, we must halt the rebellion in which we have engaged and restore the balance. Above all, we have to move from living on the edge, the periphery, and move back to the center. Ultimately, this will enable us to awaken to the spark of the universal soul within us."

There was a long silence. Jonathan tried to digest the wisdom he was gaining from Mami's explanations. The idea of man being a physical and spiritual entity seemed obvious. Drawing on his own experiences and remembering some of his mother's words before her death gave him that surety.

"Sooner or later we all have to die. We take nothing with us, son. I am at peace, because I know where I am going. You won't have to worry about me any longer," were her final words.

He was also coming to terms with man's actions and why they needed to emerge from the spirit. Yet there were some contradictions he found hard to reconcile.

Turning to Mami, Jonathan said, "But there are many actions of humans which are necessary, yet would be considered from the lower self, such as sex. How can we avoid these contradictions? Should we simply abstain? And if we did, how would the human species survive?"

Mami looked at Jonathan and quietly responded, "Sex between a man and a woman is a necessary part of the life of human beings. Quite rightly, procreation in the physical realm demands that we engage in it. However, we can encounter sex in the way the dogs you observed, casually and with numerous partners, or we can choose the right partner and commit to a monogamous relationship of marriage. In this relationship, sex is an expression of love and respect shared by two people. Furthermore, any children born are a product of that love and are brought up with the same affection. The former was motivated by lust; whereas the latter, by love, thus making it an expression of the higher self."

Jonathan was utterly surprised by such a succinct response. It is so true, he thought. There is a difference between sex driven by lust, and sex between two people who commit to fidelity and to raising a loving family. The gap, he concluded, was vast, yet, what kind of people do we have in our world who have turned sex into a ruthless business? Was there a difference between them and the animals? Dirum was right, Jonathan thought, we are animals or we are not. We make the choice.

Noticing that Gulam had dozed off into sleep, Mami stood to lay out his sleeping bag. Dirum did the same, but Jonathan continued to sit and ponder all that had been said.

He felt a true affinity to Mami. Yet, at the same time, he felt in utter awe of him.

Chapter 5

"In tears there are laughters concealed:
seek treasure amidst the ruins."[1]

The bleating of some mountain goats nearby awoke Jonathan. He turned to face the direction where he expected to see Mami in his usual morning lotus posture. What Jonathan saw instead was overwhelming. A bright rainbow adorned the sky. It was a spectacular sight as the seven colors of the rainbow tried to complete a circle, but the earth got in the way.

Mami stood gazing at this wonder, tears rolling down his cheeks. Jonathan sat up and observed Mami and the rainbow. A cold shiver ran up his spine as he noticed the momentary convergence of Mami and the rainbow.

"You are up!" Dirum proclaimed, jolting Jonathan from his contemplation.

"Yes, but look at me! I have not shaved in days. Do I look like Moses yet?" joked Jonathan.

"After last night I think you are walking in his foot-steps," Dirum answered. Jonathan felt flattered.

Dirum, Jonathan and Gulam were packed when Mami approached. Crystals of dried tears sparkled on his face the way stars do on a clear night. "Mami," Jonathan asked shyly, "what do you see in a rainbow?"

Mami looked at Jonathan sympathetically and said, "Some people look at the rainbow and it's merely a scientific phenomenon. Some people look at it as the source of great hope for the dreams they cherish. Yet others see it as a work of art by the Sustainer, and some see themselves as the rainbow. It is said that no two people see the same rainbow."

Remembering his school days and those science classes, Jonathan recalled that rainbows are formed by individual droplets of water, interacting with each other and radiating as light, which is reflected and refracted through each droplet.

Just then, Mami spoke, "When we become like the droplets of water in the rainbow, we are in harmony with the universal soul, radiating in its energy."

He did it again, thought Jonathan. He not only picked up on my thinking, but he also provided the deeper metaphor I was struggling for.

About six hours of trekking brought the group to the small village where they expected Raj and Arjun to join them. Mami spoke to the elders of the village, then rejoined the group.

"There is no indication that Raj and Arjun have arrived here," said Mami in a concerned tone. "There was talk of a rockslide in the vicinity where they were traveling."

Jonathan sat by the wayside, feeling depressed. They should have been here by now. Something must have happened. His emotion was exaggerated because he saw himself in Raj. At the first sign of a better way, a faster route, Jonathan saw himself ready to jump ship. I could have easily made the decision to accompany Raj, he thought, and memories of an incident with his financial advisor flooded his mind.

One day Jonathan had picked up the phone and called his financial advisor. Jonathan was really upset. His investment portfolio, consisting mainly of blue-chip mutual funds balanced with stocks and bonds, had not done well according to the year-end statements. His brother, Rob, had mentioned that the mutual funds his broker had recommended had appreciated thirty-two percent.

"I am really disappointed with the performance, Neil," he told his advisor. "Others are getting thirty and forty percent and my funds were up only modestly."

"We chose your portfolio based on your risk tolerance, Jonathan," Neil replied. "If I were to position your portfolio into high-growth speculative funds, it is possible to make those kind of returns, but would you accept that these types of speculative shares can also drop the same amount?"

"Well, I want faster growth," Jonathan retorted.

"Jonathan, I continue to believe that investment portfolios should be balanced between equity and income. That the equity component should consist of shares patiently acquired in companies with solid earnings and held for the long run. We should learn from the accomplishments of the great investment legends. Switching around, chasing hot funds and taking unnecessary risks will not pay over longer periods of time," pleaded Neil.

"Well, I'm moving my account," Jonathan said and hung up.

Ironically, the one thing he had learned during his time with Dirum was that progress was made with patience. He did not feel proud of having talked to Neil in that way, sounding too much like Raj and Arjun. Jonathan consoled himself by accepting that it's the kind of world we live in. Everyone is in a rush, but where are we all really going?

Do we ever stop long enough to ask? The image of lemmings falling off the cliff came to mind. If we are so unique, why do we act like them? Jonathan wondered. Society is like an octopus whose long tentacles imprison us. We can only escape by finding our own space and bringing calm into it. Mami had that when he meditated — of this much, Jonathan was convinced.

The flurry of activity by the villagers brought Jonathan back into the present. I was just like Raj and Arjun chasing short-term gains and fast results, thinking there is always a better way. There is always a price to pay for that type of thinking, Jonathan surmised, as he mulled over the huge investment losses suffered after moving his account from Neil's firm.

"What's all the commotion?" Jonathan asked Dirum, who stood nearby.

"The villagers are arranging to send a group of people to look for Arjun and Raj, and we will continue our journey," Dirum answered.

Mami and the rest of the group set off. They were within a day of arriving at their destination. Jonathan was impatient; his desire to meet Ila, the enlightened one, had grown with every step. He had so many questions, and it seemed that with each passing day, they increased. Not much was said along the way. The news of Raj and Arjun's disappearance had cast a dark shadow over everyone's mood.

About three hours into the journey, Mami called for a break. Jonathan and Dirum were very tired and they welcomed the opportunity to rest.

Gulam poured the water while Jonathan took off his shoes.

"Why?" Jonathan wondered aloud. He was feeling deeply affected. "Why did they have to go off on their own? They have never journeyed in this region before." He looked toward Mami for an answer.

"Everything happens for a reason. Let us instead learn a lesson from this and grow," Mami said.

Jonathan was not consoled. He was still agitated by the events. "Maybe we could have persuaded them," he persisted in frustration.

"I don't think so; they seemed very sure of themselves and determined," Dirum said.

The silence that followed was broken with Mami's voice as he began a story.

"There once was a village and in that village lived a very wise old man. Whenever the villagers had any questions and issues that they were not too sure of, they would go to the wise old man for his advice. However, as the children of the village grew to become young men and women, they really resented the idea of their fathers always going to the wise old man for advice. The young group gathered to discuss this matter.

'We must prove that we can do a better job with decisions than the wise old man,' they said. After awhile, they agreed that if they could prove the old man wrong, it would convince the fathers and mothers in the village that he was no longer needed. They came up with a plan and told the elders in the village that, the next day, they would prove to them once and for all that they were smarter.

Their plan was simple: in front of the elders, one of them would have a living bird in the closed palm of his hand. They would then ask the old man if the bird was dead or alive. If the old man said it was alive, the bird would be squashed before the palm was opened, proving the man wrong. Should the old man say the bird was dead, then the bird would be allowed to fly away, again proving the old man wrong.

The next day, the elders and the group of young people gathered outside the wise old man's house. As the old man emerged, he was asked the question: 'Wise old man, that which is in our hands, is it dead or alive?'

The wise old man thought for a moment and answered, 'The decision is in your hands.'"

With this, Mami peered at Jonathan and Dirum. Jonathan and Dirum sat, trying to find the meaning in the story. Mami watched for a time then continued, "In every generation, those who are younger want to assume leadership and power. This is a natural consequence because the physical laws prevail. Like the young lions that assume control of the pride, enabling it to survive, the young generation takes charge within society, enabling it to progress. The clash happens when the self-confidence within this generation reaches such an ebb that they seek to assert the same domination over issues relating to the spiritual realm. This is the clash between knowledge and wisdom."

"What's the difference?" Jonathan asked.

"Knowledge is know-how of the laws of the physical realm," Mami replied. "This is learnt mainly in schools and from books. The understanding of this knowledge enables man to survive and progress in the physical world of time and space."

"What about the inventions and discoveries that are made?" Dirum queried.

"The existence of knowledge is far more than what man has come to know," Mami told him. "Knowledge of the physical world is immense. Today we struggle to find cures for cancer and AIDS, and to find the technology to travel beyond the Milky Way, yet that knowledge already exists. However, we have not been privileged to glimpse into those aspects of the universal knowledge."

"So if the knowledge of everything already exists, where is this knowledge?" asked Jonathan. He was mystified that cures for diseases like cancer could already exist.

"In the Akashic records, my friend, this is the higher realm where the record of everything past, present and future exists," Mami responded with a smile on his face.

"So how is the knowledge available to us?" Dirum interjected, as he drew closer.

"The universal soul sustains our physical creation at all times," Mami answered. "When it wills, another aspect of creation becomes visible to us. Notice how the sun rises in the morning, bringing forth light. What man could not see at night, he was able to do by the unfolding light. Similarly, the universal soul in its own rhythm allows us glimpses of the greater knowledge. We think of these as inventions and discoveries. Yet, they are simply new chapters being introduced to us in this book called the evolution of man."

Jonathan was fascinated by what he had learnt. There was a creator—he had started to believe it—which Mami refers to as the universal soul. Surely then, this creator had the knowledge of everything. That meant that everything we discovered already existed. Mami was absolutely right! The knowledge of everything is already available and in the possession of the universal soul, deposited in the Akashic records, the sacred templates.

"So is it possible for human beings to tap into the

Akashic records and draw knowledge from it?" asked a rather excited Jonathan.

"It is limited to those who are truly enlightened," Mami answered.

"So what people have this grace?" cut in Dirum.

"There is a hierarchy with human beings, like the one that exists within the physical creation," explained Mami. "Men are like trees. Although the water with which they are nurtured is the same, their fruits are not alike. At the top of this hierarchy are enlightened people."

"Who are the enlightened ones?" Dirum asked quickly.

"They are the ones who understand the laws that operate in the spiritual realm," said Mami. "The qualities of truth, goodness, beauty, generosity, nobility and love do not occupy a remote place in their lives, but is the substance with which they nourish their spiritual being. They enjoy the light emanating from the universal soul, and while their hands are in society, their heads are cool in solitude."

"Are there enlightened ones among us?" Jonathan asked.

"Yes, there are many enlightened men and women who walk amongst us," Mami assured him. "In their presence is our own soul nourished. However, every human has the potential to be enlightened. As the highest created being, we can choose to operate from our lower self or higher spiritual self. The ability to choose is a powerful force which we possess. It gives us the free-will to be, in status, lower than the animals or higher than the angels, as shown by the prophets of the past," Mami acknowledged.

"Some people have foretold the future and continue to prophesy. Are they enlightened?" asked Jonathan, as images of cults and tarot card readers flashed before him.

Mami continued, "The material world is full of illusions. It is like a snake: its touch is soft and its bite is mortal. Those who look outside of themselves for truth shall never find it."

"I know a story I was told a long time ago," Dirum said, and he began to relate it:

"When the universal soul was creating the world, it wanted to hide the greatest treasure, the truth, in a place where it could not be abused or misused. It contemplated hiding it deep within the earth, on top of the highest mountain, in the thickest part of the forest, or even in the depth of the ocean. Finally the universal soul decided to plant the treasure of the truth deep within the human being. They could not find it there with their hands, ears or even eyes, which could only look outwards. Now the truth was safe in the world. To seek it, the human had to search deep within himself."

"That is a fitting metaphor," Mami said, as Dirum concluded his story.

"If knowledge is information of the laws of the physical world, it is, in fact, learnt knowledge. Right?" Jonathan persisted.

Mami nodded.

"So what is wisdom?"

"It is the counterpart," Mami replied. "Wisdom is knowledge of the laws of the spiritual realm. It is sometimes called revealed knowledge. It is that knowledge of the spiritual laws brought to us by the enlightened souls. It is a higher knowledge because it emanates from the realm of the infinite."

"So we already have an understanding of many of these spiritual laws," interrupted Jonathan enthusiastically.

"Yes, we do," Mami said. "Revealed knowledge gives us the understanding of spiritual laws. The very enlightened men and women and sages bring it to us. They are those elevated beings, connected to the flow of the universal soul from which they gained this knowledge. This is why it is called 'revealed.' They require understanding and study," Mami explained.

"The knowledge of these laws exists, I can see, but they are increasingly ignored in our society," Jonathan remarked.

"At our peril," Mami added.

"And what happens when knowledge and wisdom clash?" Dirum asked.

Mami answered, "The direction of society is determined by the outcome of this duel. On a macro level, a society that is overly dominated by the forces of learnt knowledge will veer. History has shown that, ultimately, they collapse. The Greek, Roman and Mongol empires, not to mention Sodom and Babylon, are good examples. When the decadence of humanity has reached epic proportions, the deterioration of the civil society is inevitable. Thus we can see that, although progress is important, if it is not chained to a spiritual foundation, it can diminish and debase the quality of human life.

"This is similar on a micro level," Mami continued. "If individuals pursue materialism from sunrise to sunset, without balancing their life with the anchor of spirituality, it will lead to despair and self-destruction. The signs of this are very evident in today's society."

Jonathan knew to what Mami was referring. His own life was a living example of the clash between knowledge and wisdom. In his case, Jonathan was quick to identify how his life had been centered on learnt knowledge, and without the calming influence of spirituality, his life had hit the wall.

"I can see how there is a bond between the physical and spiritual within creation and within each one of us," admitted Jonathan, "but when does this relationship end?"

"There are two occasions when there is a break," Mami said. "A permanent end happens at death. This is when the body returns to its origin and the soul likewise. However, it is possible to have a temporary break. This happens during moments of experience of the high when our souls can temporarily detach from the body. Sufis refer to this as, 'Die before you die.'"

"Would the near-death experience we sometimes hear about be similar?" Jonathan asked.

"Yes, these are spiritual experiences that are felt sometimes by accident, but other times by those in meditation, who are blessed," Mami finished.

The warm breeze had turned to a cold wind. The sun was nowhere to be seen and the clouds were moving around rapidly.

"We must leave now. The weather is starting to deteriorate," Mami said. He stood and picked up his pack.

By early afternoon it was snowing heavily. The last leg of the journey became more difficult, partly because of the weather and partly because the terrain was steeper. As the snow continued to fall, it was increasingly difficult to find a firm footing on the slippery slopes.

By late afternoon, Dirum, Jonathan, Gulam and Mami were caught up in a full blizzard. The blowing winds obscured visibility. About a third of the way up, Dirum slipped on the icy slope and slid thirty feet. A tree finally halted his fall. He lay in considerable pain as Mami and Jonathan rushed to his aid. The storm, meanwhile, raged on.

Mami inspected the big gash on Dirum's shin. Dirum screamed in pain at his touch. "His leg is broken," Mami shouted, trying to be heard over the howling wind.

What now, thought Jonathan; we are miles from nowhere, caught up in a freezing storm, and Dirum cannot walk. Jonathan was kneeling down by Dirum; he looked up at Mami, who stood to the side, his beard and moustache had turned white from the ice and cold. Jonathan had an eerie feeling. Mami beckoned Jonathan with a movement of his eyes, and he turned to Gulam and called him. Mami, Jonathan and Gulam huddled together, trying to protect themselves from the wind and to hear one other.

Mami spoke loudly: "Dirum cannot make it to the top alone because of his leg. If we continue without him, he will perish. Nor can we stay here, for all of us will die. The only way he can survive is if the three of us take turns supporting him by his shoulders, then perhaps he will have a chance." Without asking for help, Mami pulled Dirum up and put one of Dirum's arms around his own shoulders. He called Gulam to take the other arm.

"No!" cried Gulam. "If we do that, then all of us will slow down, and we will all perish in this storm. We have to leave him and continue; we have no choice," he protested in a panic-stricken voice.

Mami turned his eyes to Jonathan and said, "We need your shoulder."

Jonathan looked to Gulam, then to Dirum and finally to Mami. He knew this decision was the most important of his life for it concerned living or dying.

"Well, I am going on. I am not going to stay here and die," Gulam said, as he looked toward Jonathan to see whether he would accompany him.

Jonathan walked to Dirum, taking his arms, he put them over his shoulder and together the three of them struggled to continue their journey. They looked up and Gulam was gone, the distant scuffling of his feet stayed for a few moments.

The next three hours were the hardest Jonathan had ever faced. His mind and body numb from pain and cold, he dug deep within himself to find the courage and strength to continue. Step by step the three of them walked holding each other tightly so as to protect Dirum as much as possible from sudden movement.

Finally a plateau emerged. "We will rest here for a few moments. We are almost there," said Mami panting. They gently allowed Dirum to lie in a comfortable position. Mami sat with his back against the wind.

Jonathan, feeling totally exhausted, just allowed himself to fall backwards onto the snow. As he fell, his right hand hit something hard on the ground. It did not feel like a rock, so he turned his head to look while scraping the hard surface cautiously. To his horror, it was the face of Gulam. He lay there frozen. "Mami!" called Jonathan in real panic, "It is Gulam." Jonathan scraped off the remainder of the snow.

Mami came over and after checking Gulam's pulse, looked at Jonathan dejectedly and said solemnly, "He did not make it." Gulam lay there dead; Jonathan sat, frozen to the ground beside him, unable to believe his eyes. In the meantime, Mami was digging a hole in the ground. "Come help me," he called out to Jonathan. Jonathan looked over, still glued to the ground. "We have to bury him," said Mami.

Jonathan dragged himself up and shuffled over to where Mami was and began to help him dig the ground. They then carried Gulam's body and laid it in the shallow grave, filling it once again. Mami then recited some prayers and though he did not understand what was being said, Jonathan joined Mami and Dirum in the ritual.

The death of Gulam had touched a deep core within Jonathan, who was seeking some hope and comfort. Unable to contain his grief and confusion, and totally impervious to the howling cold winds, Jonathan turned to Mami and asked pointedly, "Is there a God?"

"Such are the names assigned to the universal soul. He who is above all else sustains the creation at all times with his love," responded Mami as he shielded his face from the freezing snow.

Jonathan wanted more, because he was not satisfied with a simplistic answer that there was a God who loves. Having witnessed the death of a companion he had come to like, the idea of a universal soul who cares somehow did not fit in with the mood of the moment. He had more questions; however, noticing Dirum shivering in the cold, Jonathan refrained.

"We have to go now; it is not far," Mami said as he moved to help Dirum up. Jonathan followed.

Chapter 6

*"When the Bodily Dust is gone my moon shines:
my spirit's moon finds a clear sky."*[1]

A small settlement became visible by the fires that twinkled in the dark. The noise of their arrival brought out some of the men. They were quick to take over Dirum's weight from Mami and Jonathan. Both Mami and Jonathan dropped to the ground by the fire in utter exhaustion. Quickly they started thawing as the settlers brought out some hot chai and bread. The warm blankets lent to Mami and Jonathan proved effective in helping them get back the warmth.

Jonathan, however, was visibly shaken by Gulam's death. "Why, why did he die?" he asked Mami painfully.

"Do you remember the physical laws we discussed?" Mami asked.

Jonathan thought about it for a second and said, "Yes, but if he died because of the cold weather and exhaustion, then what about us? Were we not subject to the same laws?"

Mami answered slowly. "The physical law of the cold, this we were able to overcome because by being closer to one another, the three of us created more body heat."

Surprised by the response, Jonathan probed further: "Yes, but what about the exhaustion? Surely we had a greater burden."

Once again Mami answered, "Do you remember when I told you that the laws of the spiritual realm have dominion over the physical ones?" Jonathan had a puzzled look on his face. Mami continued, "There is a spiritual law we walked in which enabled us to have a far greater capacity to endure than is ordinarily possible."

Once again Jonathan looked blank. "The spiritual laws are more certain than those you are familiar with in our physical realm," Mami said.

"Those who can see the invisible can do the impossible. Find me an instance where someone surmounted staggering odds to overcome, and I will show you from where they got the strength and courage to achieve," consoled Mami.

"Explain to me the spiritual law that saved us from exhaustion," Jonathan demanded, seeking a definitive explanation

"The law says that those who struggle and sacrifice for the welfare of others will find that their own needs are met," Mami answered.

"That means that you and I survived because we stayed to help Dirum," Jonathan gasped in astonishment.

"In every circumstance there is an opportunity. A lesson exists within any event in our lives even though we may conceive it as good or bad," Mami said.

Jonathan looked at Mami and knew that though he had participated in the expression of his higher self, it was accidental. However, for Mami, thought Jonathan, he knew all along. Not once did he try to force my decision because ultimately we can only grow when the higher self is expressed through our own volition.

Mami looked at Jonathan and said, "These spiritual laws stand before us every day, in words, in sacred texts and in the signs of nature. We have a choice. They work only when we follow them by our own free will. That is the only time we grow."

"I think Gulam was a good man. What happens to him?" Jonathan asked.

"Death is not the end," Mami said.

"I don't understand. We buried him with our own hands," Jonathan exclaimed.

"What you saw was one of the illusions that permeate the physical creation. Watch the death of the caterpillar and in this event will you see the birth of the butterfly. To the visible eye, the caterpillar died. Yet does the butterfly recognize itself when it sees the caterpillar? Do humans recognize themselves as the embryo in the womb? Similarly, unless a kernel of wheat falls to the ground and dies it remains only a single seed. But only when it dies, does it produce many seeds. In its death was new life. Observe nature and you will see a visible sign of the universal soul. Gulam's death meant the return of his body to his original state, alas in that was the freedom for his spirit to return to its origin. These are the natural laws of the spiritual realm." Jonathan remained agitated, the idea of death made him feel very uneasy.

"Death," he exclaimed. "There is so much fear of the unknown."

Mami peered upwards staring into the dark blue sky for what seemed an eternity before turning towards Jonathan sympathetically.

"As long as we live as physical beings who are only occasionally spiritual, death will continue to be a source of great despair. But when we see ourselves as spiritual beings who are temporarily human, this fear vanishes. Just as the morning mist does, in the face of the rising sun."

No sooner had Mami finished than Jonathan interjected with a question, "But the world is demanding, like an ocean whose tide is hard to resist. How do you break free from the way you have always seen yourself?"

Mami pulled the blanket around his shoulders and calmly responded, "By finding your sacred space, Jonathan, by finding your sacred space."

Jonathan lay immersed in these thoughts. He recalled the peace on his mother's face before her death. Finally he understood that she had found her sacred space. For once Jonathan could contemplate death without fear or trepidation.

Mami's gentle words stirred Jonathan out of his solitary moments, "Tomorrow, we shall wake and travel to our destination, and our journey ends. Dirum will not be able to accompany us."

Jonathan's heart reached out to Dirum as he struggled with the pain and difficulty his friend was going through. Why him? Why now? After all he was so close to reaching his goal. For this to happen now was tragic. "Why do these problems and difficulties happen in our lives?" Jonathan asked.

"They strengthen the spirit," Mami responded confidently.

Jonathan was not satisfied with the loaded statement given to him. He was searching for a more down-to-earth understanding.

Sensing this, Mami told him the following story:

"Two children began to build sand castles. One of them chose a site many yards above where the waves reached; the other built his castle close to the waves. And so when the waves came, they battered the walls, forcing him to repair them. By doing this he learnt to build a strong castle, which waves could not damage. The other child never had any contact with the waves. He never learnt to make it sturdy and strong. When the high wave came it totally destroyed the castle. Our life is like those castles. Our strength is built not by hiding from the problems of life but by facing them. Without problems, we become weaker."

Mami's story made sense to Jonathan as he reflected upon his own life. Though he really looked forward to ending the journey and having that much-anticipated meeting with Ila, the enlightened one, yet a part of him wished the end was not so close. He felt a tinge of sadness, for he could not envisage a life without Mami's shadow over him. The fire burnt brightly as Jonathan fell asleep.

Jonathan was awakened in the morning by the activity in the settlement. He observed the women walking down the valley with pails on their shoulders to fetch water. The poverty throughout his journey was the one evident fact. The other was the care and generosity of the locals. Jonathan felt sorry, especially for the children, in whose eyes he saw the reflection of his own children, Jasmin and Justin.

Mami walked to where Jonathan lay, "You weren't up early today," he said in jest.

Jonathan smiled and said, "I was just too tired."

"Mami," said Jonathan, "all this poverty brings me a lot of pain. The suffering that accompanies it, does it have to be?"

Mami was still standing. He said, "The universal soul offered the trust for our world to the mountains, but the mountains refused it. The trust was then offered to the human beings, who accepted it. I guess we have not fulfilled the trust. The fact is that on earth we have enough resources to ensure no child goes hungry. Often we blame the sustainer for the pain, misery and suffering. Yet the power to change things has been trusted in our hands."

Jonathan sat thinking about what Mami had said. It is true that if humanity wished to change things, it could. Twenty percent of the world's population consumes eighty percent of its resources. If those that have would spend just a little to help those in poverty, the story could change.

"But what about the sickness and ill health we see in the world? When we have cancer, AIDS and other diseases, people suffer and no one can help them," Jonathan stated.

Mami waited a few moments before responding. "We live in a perishable world. Every living thing has to pass through the doors of death. Every healthy person shall be visited by sorrow, disease and ill health at some time. Such are the seasons ordained in our perceptible world. Yet within these sharp turns in our lives are lessons. Trust in them, just as a snake does on losing its skin, or the sheep that sacrifices its wool. The destiny of the being within us is infinitely more important than the worldly difficulties we sometimes have to endure. The body in sickness conforms to the natural laws of the physical world, alas in this is the spirit strengthened."

These words left a deep impression on Jonathan. It was true. Everyone faces hardships in their lives. Often people fall into the trap of self-pity. Yet almost always such situations create great turns and changes that impact not just the person affected but also those around them. Life does present rare opportunities for people to respond with courage, compassion and selfless sacrifice. Jonathan concluded that our responses are all we control, yet in them is our destiny shaped. Reflecting further he saw vivid pictures of the distress in Western society. The pain and baggage from previous hurts and past emotional traumas cling like leeches sucking the very life out of people, draining away their vitality and zest for living. "Mami," Jonathan asked after a moment, "so many people live without purpose, weighed down by the scars of the past. Can they heal themselves? Could they find lasting happiness?"

Mami sat silently awhile, then responded rather sadly. "This is a plight that is not exclusive to the West. Rather, it is the outcome of a civilization whose participants are increasingly becoming techno-human, a humanism of sorts devoid of spirituality." Mami paused, thinking deeply. He stood up and peered at Jonathan. "Find the spirit, for in this is the elixir of healing and happiness." With these words Mami left to pick up his belongings.

Mami's response had opened an old wound. After much soul searching, Jonathan realized that the idealism of his youth was not a phantom, but a calling whose time had arrived. Jonathan packed his things and went to visit Dirum, who was being cared for in one of the small brick houses. In the bright daylight the settlement seemed much bigger than at night. There must have been at least four hundred homes in the village. In the middle was a marketplace.

Dirum was really happy to see Jonathan. "Thank you very much," said Dirum as he gave Jonathan an affectionate hug. Jonathan sat with Dirum for a while and told him that he was going to go on. "I will return here on my way back," he assured him. "And, oh, make sure you are walking, I am not planning to carry you down that hill," he finished with a grin on his face.

As Jonathan left the house, he heard Dirum's voice echo through the window, "Khudha hafiz." Jonathan knew what it meant and it pleased him.

Mami and Jonathan set off on what was to be a two-hour trek. Mami seemed in an unusually affectionate mood and gave Jonathan the opportunity to ask some questions that particularly bothered him. "There is so much unhappiness in the world, how do people overcome this?" Jonathan asked as he walked beside Mami.

"Happiness is not a product you buy, nor is it a place you get to. But it is a feeling," Mami said.

"Then how can you feel happy?" asked Jonathan.

"In the illusionary world, we mistake gratification with happiness. Yet happiness is a state of being when our essence is in harmony with the universal soul," Mami replied.

"Then tell me about the universal soul. And how can our essence be in harmony with it?" Jonathan inquired with deep interest.

"The universal soul is that which has created everything visible and that which is invisible. It continues to sustain this creation at all times. Its energy is continually flowing within this creation in every atom and every particle. Nature is the only visible sign of the universal soul. It has a perfect balance: the cycle of the seasons, the orbits of the sun and the moon, the tides of the oceans, the fall of the rain, and the alternation of day and night. Contemplate the beauty in nature, in a single flower; and observe how a bee fertilizes the flower, which it robs. Watch how birth becomes death and its subsequent emergence as life. Reflect on how a tree laden with fruit has its branches bowed to earth in humility, yet the barren one stands in arrogance. If you wish to see the universal soul then it is only visible through its handiwork, nature. However the greatest of all treasures is the everlasting nobility of the human soul, the essence, through this alone can we feel the energy of the universal soul. When men and women live in harmony within spiritual laws, they will experience the universal soul, in all its glory and magnificence. They will be effervescent in its flow and feel the happiness they seek," Mami finished as he stopped and looked at Jonathan, who had never heard Mami talk in this way. It was as a father would give his last advice to a son.

It sounded like a good-bye, Jonathan felt that, and he did not want it to end. "How am I going to experience the universal soul?" Jonathan asked feeling a creeping fear.

"Find the precious seeds, plant them and be sure to nourish them," Mami clarified.

"But how can I be certain of what I find?" Jonathan quickly asked.

Mami thought about it carefully before he spoke. "The highest level of certainty can only come with direct experience. Consider a moth, which is attracted to the light of the naked flame. It craves to be one with the light because such is its nature. It will instinctively get attracted to it when it approaches the light. The moth has the vision of it, but vision can be an illusion. As it gets closer it can feel the heat, but feelings can be misleading. Only when the moth is annihilated in the flame will it truly experience the light. Similarly when you have found, planted and nourished the precious seeds, your experience will be your certainty," Mami concluded, leaving Jonathan the impression in no uncertain terms that they would be his final words.

Jonathan was overcome, he did not want to let go, he did not want to say good-bye, and he couldn't. He looked at Mami with a pained look.

Mami came closer. "I will always be with you, as you with me." With that he put his arms around Jonathan and embraced him, patting his shoulder numerous times and saying, "May you be blessed."

Jonathan stood motionless; teardrops formed around his eyes as Mami slowly faded away into the distance. The sound of his voice kept ringing in Jonathan's ears: "I will always be with you as you with me." He listened again and again, afraid to move, afraid to miss a single beat.

In the valley below he could see a small settlement, and he began to walk toward it. As he arrived, he asked one of the vendors in the small marketplace where he could find Ila, the enlightened one. They pointed further down the valley where the two rivers met.

Twenty minutes later Jonathan saw a small meadow; a makeshift and temporary structure had been erected with a canopy over it. There were about one hundred people seated in front of a raised platform, decorated in red and green.

Jonathan went to one of those seated toward the end and asked of Ila. "Yes, he will come, we are all awaiting him," the stranger responded gently.

Jonathan looked at the small crowd that was seated in patience. They were chanting some words he had not heard before. At the back of the structure was a large kiosk a vendor had set up. He sold water and some local food made of potatoes and bread. A small group stood there, drinking, eating and chatting. Jonathan bought himself some water for his thirst.

The man to his left reached to him politely. "Are you American?" he asked.

"No, I am Canadian," Jonathan responded.

"You have come a long way?" he asked again.

"Yes, I flew to Islamabad, took the bus to Gilgit, then we drove to Hunza, from where I walked," Jonathan answered.

"My name is Badakshan. I am here with my father and brother," he said, pointing to an old man who appeared to be at least seventy, standing by another man half his age.

"So where have you come from?" Jonathan inquired.

"We have come from Afghanistan," Badakshan answered.

"So which route did you take?" asked Jonathan, hoping to gain some information about the travel routes in the region.

"We walked from Kabul," came the answer.

Jonathan was a little puzzled. Based on his knowledge of geography, Afghanistan was a bordering country to the northwest. It must be hundreds of kilometres away. Did they really walk all that distance? How could such an old man undertake a journey of this nature? And the purpose was to meet Ila the enlightened one, thought Jonathan. "How long did it take?" he asked.

"Thirty-two days," answered Badakshan.

"You have traveled all that distance to see Ila, the enlightened one? You must have a lot of questions for him," Jonathan said, feeling that he was not alone in his quest for answers.

"We don't have any questions," Badakshan said.

Jonathan peered at Badakshan in surprise and asked, "Then why do you want to meet him?"

"To have didar," he responded.

Jonathan was familiar with that word. Dirum had used it. It was the opportunity to have the energy from an enlightened soul radiate within one's own, thereby cleansing the mirror of one's own soul. Is this worth all the sacrifices such travelers had made, wondered Jonathan silently. Soon Jonathan joined this small crowd and sat with them. They sat in contemplation, continuing to chant and recite what he was told were words from their sacred texts. He became very comfortable in the rhythm. The evening wore on and it started to get dark. There was no electricity, however, three small fires were kept burning. Jonathan had become completely relaxed; he was at the end of his journey awaiting he who would give him the missing piece to his puzzle. That mood of peace permeated the entire crowd; it seemed everyone was there for the same reason. The one mindedness of the group had an uncanny calming influence upon Jonathan. He felt a sense of inner silence that made him forget everything. Suddenly he felt the energy as the crowd increased the rhythm and tempo of the chanting. It was as if something was happening.

A cold breeze blew into the structure, as Jonathan observed the entrance of the man called Ila, the enlightened one. It was dark; his face was not visible under his cape. Jonathan watched him sit on the raised platform whilst the small group sat in pin-drop silence. After a few moments Ila spoke very gently. Jonathan did not understand the words but he felt the sentiments. After a couple of minutes, Ila ended his words with the recitation of some blessings to which Jonathan joined the group in responding with an amen. The next few minutes were the most unique Jonathan had ever experienced. He sat in silence and felt a sense of being that was totally alien. A peaceful feeling of tranquility and oneness overcame Jonathan. For a moment he did not know who he was or why he had even come here. He felt alive in the moment, which he did not wish to surrender. He began to understand what Dirum meant by didar and why people journeyed for this nectar. Then one by one the devotees stood. They walked humbly to Ila, where they received his blessing. Without looking back, they left the structure. It was Jonathan's turn. This was the purpose of his journey, the object of all his sacrifices. He had prepared and practiced his questions a million times. This was his time, the only time and now the answers were at hand. He walked toward Ila, whose face he could not see; he lowered his head in humility. Ila put his hand on Jonathan's shoulder. Jonathan felt an energy that was overwhelming yet familiar. His mind was numb yet at peace. Jonathan's mouth would not respond, no questions flowed from it, at that moment they seemed trivial. Ila spent an unusually long time blessing Jonathan.

At the end of it Ila spoke gently, and said, "The jewels of the rainbow contain what you seek. Let them find you."

Jonathan emerged from the structure without turning back. An inertia and magnetism drew him away from Ila's energy, despite his resistance. He kept walking toward the village, impervious to his surroundings.

In the village, Jonathan wandered around, not knowing what to do or where to turn in the commotion of the marketplace.

Some words from one of the vendors caught his attention: "The seven jewels of the rainbow here."

Jonathan turned and inquired. The vendor had numerous pouches; each contained seven colored stones, each representing a color from the rainbow. "They bring good luck, only sixty-two rupees," the vendor said.

Jonathan dug into his belt, pulled out some rupees and bought a pouch, then he continued to wander. His mind stayed numb. It was as if he had been hit by lightning, unable to either think straight or rationalize, engrossed in the moment he had experienced, a moment in which he had felt a connection to his very essence. Jonathan continued to walk aimlessly in the dark, past the din of the village and into the thick of the night.

Chapter 7

"The spirit is wanting in that resplendent form:
go seek that jewel rarely found!"[1]

Stumbling along in the dark, Jonathan had inadvertently wandered toward the edge of the nearby hilltop. The loose stones started to give way under the weight of his feet and Jonathan began to slide down the hillside. He rolled for some ten metres desperately trying to hold on to anything that would stop his fall. Noticing a large branch, Jonathan lunged and grabbed it and for a moment he held on dangling with one hand. Pulling the other hand up, he was now able to get both hands onto the branch.

He looked up and saw an impossible incline. So he glanced down hoping for a way out. The sweat on his forehead dripped rapidly when he could not see the bottom.

"Help," Jonathan shouted numerous times. "Is there someone up there? Help!" In the silence of the night, his voice echoed. He shouted again, "Help me, please, someone. I can't hold on, it is a hundred feet down, someone please help." The echo once again returned, mimicking his call for help. Jonathan's hands were weakening; he knew he could not hold on for much longer.

"Do you believe in the universal soul?"

For a moment Jonathan was surprised by the voice, but he answered immediately,

"Yes, yes, I believe in the universal soul, now please can you help? I can't hang on, my arms are weakening, could you please help me?"

The voice returned, "Do you trust the universal soul?" it asked.

Jonathan replied quickly in a panic-stricken tone, "Yes, I trust, I trust the universal soul, but I am weakening and I can't hang on! Please help me."

The voice returned, "Then let go!"

Jonathan was taken back for a moment. He was in fear and at the depth of despair. He hung in silence, as his past flashed before him. The face of Mami emerged before him and he remembered his words, "If you trust in the universal soul as you should, he would sustain you as he does the bird which in the morning goes forth hungry." Jonathan chose to trust, so he let go. He began to drop, and within seconds a ledge below broke his fall. He screamed with pain as his ankle caught awkwardly. For a few moments Jonathan sat there, holding his ankle.

The sound of thunder in the sky was followed by rain. Noticing a cave-like gap by the ledge, Jonathan crawled inside. The rain teemed down relentlessly as he peered out of the cave in relief. Suddenly, he was startled by a loud thunderous noise accompanied by the sound of falling rocks. It was a rockslide, and Jonathan looked out in horror as the falling mud and rocks slowly covered his window to the world. Frantically he tried to claw away the debris, to no avail. There was just too much mud.

It was pitch black inside the cave. Jonathan sat in the corner; he could not tell whether his eyes were open or closed. Without a choice he was drawn into contemplation. He remembered Mami's words that "the secret of everything was to be in the same flow as the universal soul," but first he had to find the precious seeds. What are these precious seeds? Where do I find them? wondered

Jonathan as his mind drifted to the thoughts of Ila, the enlightened one. Who was he? And what did he mean when he said that, "The jewels of the rainbow contain what you seek; let them find you."

Time passed as Jonathan meditated on these thoughts. Neither hunger nor fear drew close as he sat in concentration, not through choice but because of circumstance. Minutes, then hours drifted away.

A green shimmering light on the floor of the cave caught Jonathan's eye. It must have been the first thing he saw in a long time. He rubbed his eyes to make sure it was real. Slowly Jonathan moved, crawling toward the light. As he drew closer, he realized that the green sparkling light was that of one of the stones he had purchased from the marketplace. A ray of light was entering the cave and illuminating the green stone as it lay on the floor beside the pouch. For a moment Jonathan just sat staring at the shining green stone. After some thirty-six hours in meditation the green jewel was the first thing he saw. His heart began to beat faster as he realized that he had discovered the first jewel of the rainbow; it was meditation, which was the green of the rainbow. He stood up, acknowledging that Ila was right, the jewel had actually found him. In that epiphanic moment he followed the thin ray of light to the mouth of the cave and began to push out the mud. It was not that difficult.

The torrent of rain had continued endlessly, washing down more rocks and mud, clearing the accumulation on the ledge. He staggered out, limping on one foot. Jonathan looked up and, to his relief, the fallen rocks had paved the way for him to climb back up. Picking up his pouch of colored stones, he stepped out into the light one more time and slowly began the climb to the top.

Once there, Jonathan began limping back toward the valley. His ankle was very painful and his pace was slow. He stopped at the side of the dirt track lifting his leg to take a closer look at the ankle in the light of day. It did not look good. It was swollen to the size of a baseball and, worst of all, it was throbbing very painfully. Jonathan was raised to be strong and proud. "You have to be tough and never show people you are weak," his father used to say. He picked up a long stick and continued to walk. The odd passers by could never have guessed the burden Jonathan carried, nor did he ask for any assistance. Seeking help meant being inferior and not self-sufficient. "I can make it on my own," Jonathan thought to himself.

By late afternoon, the blood in his ankle was no longer circulating properly, he could no longer put any weight on it, and so Jonathan decided to sit by the side of the road. He was hungry and unable to continue, but he told himself, I will be better soon, then I will resume. As Jonathan sat by the side of the road, many wayfarers passed, as did time, but his ankle did not get better. Numerous times he tried to stand, but was forced to take the weight off the leg.

It was starting to get cool in the early evening. Jonathan was weak from hunger and tired from his ordeal. He watched as a young ten-year-old boy came up the path.

"Hey! You speak English?" the boy called.

"I do," answered Jonathan.

The boy drew closer, and with a mischievous grin and broken words he said, "I am learning English, my name is Sachu." Sachu was talkative, it was not often he got a chance to practice his English and Jonathan seemed the perfect candidate. "Why you sit here?" Sachu asked.

"I have hurt my ankle," said Jonathan who appreciated the boy's concern.

"Show me," he demanded.

Sachu looked and winced, "Boy-oh-boy, that is not good. You want me to bring help?" he inquired sincerely.

"No, no I can handle it. It will get better soon."

"Okay, I am going," said the boy abruptly. As he began to hop away, he shouted. "My papa was right. Some people are too proud."

Jonathan sat silently as he watched the young boy go around the corner. Many thoughts crossed his mind, especially of the green of the rainbow. Meditation was how Mami always started and ended his day. Somehow he seemed to draw so much energy from it.

The sunlight was now almost gone. Jonathan's parched lips, fatigue and hunger pains were making him doubt his own judgment. I should have asked someone to help me, he thought. It would soon be dark, his leg was not getting better and surviving a night outside in his condition seemed dangerous. He kept seeing the images of the boy skipping away and his words kept echoing back from the valley below. "My papa was right. Some people are too proud."

Sachu was right, thought Jonathan as he looked up into the sky. I am too proud; my pride has got me into this mess. And as he came to that conclusion he noticed the red glow above. To his amazement the whole sky was like a red canopy. Jonathan realized that the red jewel of the rainbow had just found him. It was pride. Memories came back in a flood. He was returning to his office after lunch with some clients. It was a nice day and he had walked.

On the side of the road were some panhandlers, and Jonathan remembered that he never tossed a dime, though many had their palms raised. Don't they have any pride? Why can't they go get a job, he used to think. They are just lazy, he had assumed. Now he sat on the side of the road, and his plight no different. Avoiding pride, he thought, as he gazed into the sky in wonderment, was the red jewel of the rainbow.

In the distance Jonathan heard hoofbeats; it sounded like a horse pulling a wagon. As it drew closer, he noticed that it was two cows pulling a cart. Things are rarely what they seem, he thought. As the cart came by, instinctively Jonathan raised his arms and cried out, "Can you please help me!"

The cart stopped and an old man stepped out. He walked to where Jonathan sat and with one look at his ankle, he gave out a shout. A woman, who appeared to be his wife, got down from the cart, and without any words the couple lifted Jonathan into the cart and continued on their way. Jonathan fell asleep under the cover of the red sky.

Chapter 8

*"You held a blue glass before your eye:
for that reason the world seemed to you to be blue."*[1]

When Jonathan awoke, he lay in a small wooden bed, in what looked like a very small brick house. There were no other rooms, and it became apparent that everyone in this family slept here.

Looking around, Jonathan surmised that the occupants lived a poor and meager existence. Just as he turned sideways, he noticed that his fanny pack, which had the last of his rupees, was gone. In a state of panic, Jonathan raised his arm to find that his Rolex too had disappeared. I have been robbed, he thought. They have taken everything I have. Am I safe here? he wondered.

Just then an old man entered the room, he remembered him from the night before. His face had countless scars and wrinkles. Jonathan thought he must be a hardened criminal from his appearance. "How are you?" he asked in a heavy voice and broken English.

"Thank you for helping me," said Jonathan, fearing what was next.

"Your leg very bad, three days," he said, showing three fingers.

Jonathan did not quite understand what the old man meant and looked at him puzzled. "No walk, three days," said the old man, noticing the expression on his face.

Just than the old woman walked into the room with a saucepan in her hand. She gently lifted Jonathan's leg and put it on her lap. Using her hand she scooped up a strong smelling orange paste and carefully applied it on Jonathan's swollen ankle. She disappeared and returned with another pan. Carefully lifting Jonathan's head, she slid her hand under the head and began to feed him some soup. It was the first thing he had eaten in days and he just devoured it. At this time the old man returned. In his hand were Jonathan's belongings, which he placed by his side and left. The old woman finished feeding him and disappeared too.

Jonathan was left alone once again. He tried to figure out what had just happened. Staring at the orange paste plastered all over his ankle, Jonathan felt rather ashamed of himself. I condemned them. I branded them as criminals. They helped me when I needed help. Without a word, selflessly they sacrificed, he thought to himself. How could I do that, he asked himself. They don't even know me. I am just a stranger yet they took me in, shared with me all that they have, and I branded them. In my mind I tried and convicted them. How could I have been so judgmental he thought as he sought to move his leg?

The pain was excruciating, as he reached out to steady his leg. The orange of the paste was now on his fingers, and the expression on his face changed, as he knew that the orange jewel of the Rainbow had found him — Non Judgmental. Jonathan sat there in disbelief, realizing that being judgmental was always one of his worst habits. His mind wandered back to the panhandlers. He judged them to be lazy and no good, yet everyone faces his own circumstances, he thought. Surely the kind old man could have thought the same of me. It seems that we are all guilty of this. We see others and if they are different, in

color, language, culture or even appearance, our judgments create prejudices. These are surely the roots of
conflicts in society. There is immense diversity in the
world, yet does it have to be a source of weakness?
Jonathan recalled visiting the Grand Canyon with his
parents. Though quite young he remembered the boat
excursion along the Canyon River. The huge walls scaled
the skies with ever-changing colors and textures. Green,
yellow, black, brown and white intermingling with soft,
rough and glazed textures. Together they had created one
of the natural wonders of the world. Diversity too is a
great wonder and strength, concluded Jonathan, but only
when we are non judgmental. Alas, we make judgments
based on the limited knowledge of the real. We look at life
through a keyhole believing that to be the whole view.

Chapter 9

"He who gave water to the rivers and fountains
hath opened a fountain within me."[1]

*I*n the morning Jonathan awoke feeling physically much stronger, although his ankle continued to be rather painful. At around midday the old man appeared at the house accompanied by another. Jonathan turned on his bed curiously. It was Dirum.

"Jonathan," he exclaimed as he walked briskly over.

"I am so glad to see you," Jonathan said as they embraced. This was the same village Dirum had stayed behind to recover from his broken leg. "I did not have a clue where I was, what a coincidence," Jonathan said. Dirum looked at Jonathan with raised eyebrows. "Okay, okay, there are no coincidences. Everything happens for a reason," Jonathan corrected himself as Dirum smiled.

"I see you have the orange paste on your ankle. I do too," said Dirum lifting his leg, which revealed an orange tan beneath the bandaged shin.

"What is it?" Jonathan asked.

"It is turmeric; it's a strong spice that works wonders in healing the body. I think we can learn a lot from these natural medicines," Dirum answered.

Over the next two hours, Jonathan and Dirum got caught up with all that had happened. As expected, Jonathan did most of the talking.

"Tell me about the seven jewels, of the rainbow again, and this time, go slowly and do not miss anything. But first, start with Mami," Dirum said.

"Before Mami left he had said to me that those who were enlightened knew the purpose of life and how to achieve happiness. So I had asked him how one became enlightened. His answer was that the universal soul continuously emanated energy, and those who could live in the flow of its spiritual energy were enlightened because of it. When I had asked him how, he simply said, find the precious seeds, plant and nourish them. But why are you so interested in what Mami said?" Jonathan inquired.

"I will tell you later," Dirum replied.

Jonathan continued, "In Ila's presence I felt so emancipated. I was not Jonathan, but I was, and I felt my real self. It was truly a profound experience that I don't have words for. It's funny. I was always looking for answers. My whole objective was to just get to Ila, the enlightened one, get the answers and go home. Yet when I was there I could not speak, I had no questions, nothing really mattered except the moment, which I cherished. Ila made me worthless, yet oh so precious. I just cannot explain. I realize that the answers we seek are found in life's lessons. For life is a journey of self-discovery."

Dirum sat in silence listening. His eyes were moist; with every word, Dirum relived Jonathan's experience as if it were his own. Jonathan continued, "As I was leaving, Ila the enlightened one spoke to me. He said, 'The jewels of the rainbow contain what you seek; let them find you.'"

Dirum listened and stayed silent as Jonathan concluded with the three jewels that had found him. "Well," said Jonathan, looking at Dirum to provide some insight.

He looked Jonathan straight in the eye and said, "I do not know whether you will believe what I am going to tell you." Jonathan's eyes opened wide as Dirum spoke. "Mami, and Ila, the enlightened one, were one and the same."

"What!" Jonathan exclaimed. "I knew it! That is what I felt, those deja vu experiences, numerous times. From the beginning Mami touched a chord in me, and that time in Ila's presence, I felt the same part of me come alive. But how did you know?"

"Well," Dirum answered, "that day before you left, Mami came to me to say goodbye. Sensing how disappointed I was at not having the opportunity to get didar of Ila the enlightened one, he put his hand on my forehead and said, 'That which you seek has already been granted unto you.' That night I had a dream that I sat in a meadow and the enlightened one came and blessed me. I looked up and the face I saw was Mami's," finished Dirum.

"It was in a meadow," Jonathan said rather excitedly. "All this time he was with us and yet we looked elsewhere. Is it not always the case, sometimes we look for things yet we already have them? The grass is always greener on the other side. But why do you think he concealed this?"

Shaking his head in amazement, Dirum said, "I believe that he wanted to leave a valuable lesson for us. One that we would not forget. That the difference between the outward form and inner essence could only be discerned through personal experience." Jonathan waited for Dirum to continue.

"What we seek is always with us, yet we are sometimes blind to it. I don't think we will ever forget this." After a brief moment of silence, Dirum exclaimed. "Well, we still need to discover the seven jewels of the Rainbow, for surely they will provide the answers everyone seeks."

"You are right Dirum, every human ultimately asks what is the meaning of life and how can we achieve true and lasting happiness. This is what people live for, strive and struggle toward," Jonathan deduced.

"Well, you already have three of them. The green is meditation, the red is to avoid pride, and orange is to be non-judgmental. Alas, there are seven colors in the rainbow," Dirum added.

Jonathan reached into his pocket and pulled out the pouch and revealed the colored stones. "Yes, we still need to find violet, blue, yellow and indigo, but Mami had said that they will find us," said Jonathan thoughtfully.

The next day, Jonathan's ankle was a little better. The swelling had gone down and he could walk slowly with the use of a walking stick. Dirum too was quite mobile. Although he had a plaster of sorts around his shin, he was able to walk with the use of a cane. They spent the day outdoors, wandering around the marketplace and chatting with locals whom they got to know quite well. Both Dirum and Jonathan's hosts had many things in common. They were poor and lived a life of subsistence. The husbands worked in the fields and the wives took care of the home, and children, and fetched water. Despite this they were warm and caring people who selflessly offered to share what they had.

Jonathan pondered deeply about life and remarked, "Each day the deer awakes knowing that he has to run faster than a lion in order to survive the day. Each day the lion awakes knowing that he has to be more cunning if he is to catch the deer, for without food he knows he cannot survive. I used to live a similar life, where each day like millions, I drove to work knowing that in order to earn my paycheck I had to win. I lived an animal's existence, yet I find that the people here are so refreshingly down to earth. They struggle and life is indeed harsh, yet I don't see that 'dog eat dog' attitude, so common in the so-called civilized societies."

Dirum watched and nodded in agreement. "You have really changed," he complimented Jonathan.

"What do you mean?"

"They say that our thoughts became our words and these words became our deeds. What we say is a reflection of what we are. You are truly discovering your own nobility," answered Dirum with a sincere tone.

Jonathan felt flattered by his comments. He had come to despise his superficial character, and his experiences were enabling him to break out of the crust of ignorance that surrounded him to finally discover his true self. "But how do you control the quality of your thoughts when sometimes my thoughts are so petty?" asked Jonathan.

Dirum did not answer. Changing the subject he spoke sadly, "Mami said to me before he left that he would always be with me."

"Me, too," said Jonathan, equally downcast. "I really do feel him close to me, yet I know you do too, and so do countless others! How is that possible?"

"Love is like that, the more of it you give, the more you have," Dirum reflected, as he began to recite a verse from Omar Khayyam's Rubaiyat.

Ah love could you and I with him conspire
to grasp this sorry scheme of things entire,
Would not we shatter it to bits and then remould it
Nearer to the heart's desire!

The second day at the village passed in a similar way with Dirum and Jonathan finding plenty of time to converse and observe life in the foothills of the Himalayas, in these Northern areas of Pakistan. By the third day both Jonathan and Dirum were much more mobile and were wandering around the village without any aids. At noon they stopped at the vendor selling bread in the market. They bought a large loaf to share between them. Jonathan sat on a rock awaiting Dirum to join him. Dirum instead had moved under the shade of a large tree and waved to Jonathan to join him there.

"Let us eat under here. It's wise to avoid the midday heat of the bright sun," said Dirum loudly.

Jonathan understood. Throughout the journey they had tried to avoid the heat of the sun at midday. That is the time it seemed hottest. They sat in the shade as Jonathan broke the loaf into half. Food was scarce and so were Jonathan's and Dirum's resources.

They tried to conserve what they had by having just one meal each day. Jonathan took a bite; however, before Dirum could, the wailing of a child distracted him. He consoled the child and gave her a part of his bread. But the little girl continued to cry. Dirum talked to her for a moment, than gave the girl the rest of the bread. Immediately the girl ran off into the alley. "What was all that about?" Jonathan inquired.

"Well, at first I thought the little girl was hungry, so I gave her some of my bread. But then I found out that the reason for her tears was that her father was at home ill and that he too had not eaten. So I gave her the rest of my bread for her family," Dirum answered sympathetically.

Jonathan was very touched by Dirum's act of kindness

and generosity, and without thinking twice; he broke his bread in half and gave it to Dirum. Just as he did that the sun burst through the leaves temporarily blinding him. Jonathan stood to move and froze with the image of the yellow jewel of the Rainbow.

"It is generosity!" shouted Jonathan in excitement. "The yellow jewel of the rainbow is generosity. You are an inspiration, Dirum."

Dirum, meanwhile, stared at his friend in disbelief as he remembered Mami's words, "Allow the best in you to emerge, for this is the way to the higher self."

Later that afternoon, Dirum and Jonathan sat overlooking the valley below, watching the beautiful work of art it was. "If all the women did not have to spend so much time each day just fetching water, wouldn't life become very different?" asked Jonathan as he observed a group of young girls walking down to the valley's floor to fetch water from the river.

"Well, it would certainly allow them the time to do other things," Dirum said.

"Like what for instance?" he asked.

Dirum thought about it for a moment and said, "Well, maybe they could set up community schools to teach the children, or become more involved in health care matters, or maybe just help their husbands in work. Either way, it would contribute to increasing their quality of life."

"My heart, however, really goes out to the young children. They grow up, yet there is nothing for them to do. There are no schools, nor any other activity. They could become so much more if an investment of time and resources was made in their education, mentoring and coaching. It is just tragic."

"A little thing like water, which we take for granted. Just turn the tap, that's all we do. Water on demand, do we appreciate that? Water is life!" Jonathan said pointedly.

"The only time you appreciate anything, is when you do not have it," responded Dirum.

"Yes, or when you have had to struggle to get it; then you would know its value," added Jonathan.

After a moment's silence, Jonathan asked, "What do you think it would cost to build a small canal that would reroute water from one of the upper rivers to go past this village?"

Dirum thought about that for quite a while. Then he said, "About six-hundred-thousand rupees, I guess. Especially since you could get the villagers to do a large part of the labor. So all you need is the engineering and materials like dynamite. Fortunately the main river is not far."

"How much would that be in U.S. dollars?" Jonathan inquired.

"I guess about nine thousand dollars," Dirum responded with a quick calculation.

I have spent more than this at the casinos in Vegas, and lost even more in the stock market, Jonathan thought rather shamefully. "Mami was right, all the resources exist within this planet of ours to ensure no one goes to bed hungry at night, that no child has to die because of a preventable disease. If we are such an advanced race then why do we allow this to happen?" questioned Jonathan disappointedly.

"We are a race, yet everyone is not equal. There is a hierarchy even within human beings," Dirum answered.

"If within the animal existence, the hierarchy goes from the weakest to the strongest, what about in humans?" Jonathan asked.

"Within humans, the hierarchy goes from ignorance to enlightenment. We do not have an instrument that measures the spirituality in each soul. It is seen only in the actions and character of man. Like Mami would say, 'You know a tree by the fruit it bears.' However, since we still have so many problems on our planet, it tells you something," concluded Dirum.

"When that old man in the market—you know, the one who sells the bread—when he asked me, 'If man can go to the moon, why can't my daughter go to school?', I figured we have a long way to go," Jonathan said, as he drifted off into his thoughts.

As the sun began to set, Dirum and Jonathan walked back to the village. Some familiar faces of the vendors at the market greeted them. As they stopped to get a cup of chai, one of the more prominent members of the village came over and had a short conversation with Dirum.

Jonathan watched his friend's face light up and asked, "What did he say?"

"Good news, there is a horse wagon leaving for Gilgit tomorrow to pick up supplies for the village. Since it will be empty, we can get a ride," Dirum said rather excitedly.

Jonathan could not contain his emotions at the news. Without a ride, he would have had to wait at least another week before undertaking the long trip back. That evening Jonathan and Dirum sat with the villagers who had organized a farewell gathering. The fire burnt brightly and their hosts seemed genuinely sad to see them go. To Dirum's amazement, Jonathan stood and approached the prominent elders. He removed his Rolex and gave it to one of them. The Elderly man looked up wondering why Jonathan was giving him the gift.

"This is a Rolex," Jonathan said. "You can sell it in the city for about nine thousand dollars. I would be honored if you could use that money to build a canal passing by your village."

The old man just looked at Jonathan, and then he stood up with tears in his eyes and gave him a huge embrace. The elderly man addressed the rest of the villagers who were all wondering what was going on.

A frenzy of humming could be felt as they heard the news, and before long, there was rejoicing in the streets. Out of the homes poured out musicians, and the children who had been tucked into bed. In the meanwhile the villagers scrambled to hug and kiss Jonathan. The rejoicing continued late into the night. The impact of having clear water so readily accessible would permanently change the quality of life of everyone who lived in these very difficult conditions.

"I would never have expected a gesture like that from you," Dirum admitted as he sat down by the fire.

"I am not the person I was," Jonathan confessed.

"You loved that watch," said Dirum.

Jonathan thought about how he had cherished the watch. He almost had a heart attack when it had fallen in the lake. "I can buy replicas of that watch in New York for twenty dollars. No one would know," Jonathan answered.

"What you have done will truly make a difference here," Dirum praised.

"I really thought about it," Jonathan continued. "Yesterday I saw an old man who could barely walk. He was planting something. Noticing the pain and effort he was making I asked if I could help. He gave me some seeds to plant, and I asked him what they were. He said they were apple seeds. Since it takes a good many years for an apple tree to bear fruit, I asked him why, thinking to myself he would never taste them. To my surprise the old man said that he had never tasted an apple; however, he was going to make sure that his grandchildren did. It got me thinking that people struggle and strive in every society, yet I also realized that as a civilization, if we are so advanced and educated why are we not putting our intellect into the service of mankind. We live like animals though we realize it not. Life was always about taking care of me. We club each other along the way, and every creature we see acts in this way. Mami was so right, we are infinitely more than we realize. In any case, you never have anything unless you give a part of it away. I feel so good about what I did," Jonathan surmised.

Dirum wondered for a moment and said, "A True King is one who has gained the love and respect of the poor, and you have done that today."

Chapter 10

"The undisciplined man does not maltreat himself alone, but he sets the whole world on fire."[1]

Jonathan and Dirum loaded up the wagon with their belongings, and to their surprise, the whole village stood to say goodbye. The villagers recited some prayers for their guests' safe journey, after which they were presented with a parting gift.

After the goodbyes they climbed into the empty wagon, which was hitched to a beautiful horse. The driver introduced himself as Salman. He was a young and jolly fellow. "How long will it take us to get to Gilgit?" Jonathan asked.

"One night and two days," Salman said, keeping his eye on the path. The route they took was different. In order to avoid the steep slopes, they took the longer trail. They would still be there in less than half the time. Relieved that he did not have to make the long hike on a weak ankle, Jonathan sighed in relief as the horse began to trot.

"Dirum, do you believe prayers really work? I know they bring people hope, but at the end of it all is there really something in this?" Jonathan asked as vivid images of the doctor's words asking him to pray for Jasmin became intermingled with those of the villagers praying for his safe journey and of Mami as he recited those prayers on burying Gulam.

"Do you remember Mami telling us that we are a microcosm of the universal soul?" Dirum asked looking for validation. Jonathan nodded approvingly. "If we are made up of the same substance as that of the universal soul, then surely our words, thoughts and prayers carry immense weight within the macrocosm," Dirum concluded emphatically.

"I never thought of it that way. You are right, our words have strength," exclaimed Jonathan. "Prayers are acts of goodwill, generosity and compassion coming from our higher self. They are expressions of our deepest spirituality. In them are others assisted, and our own essence uplifted," ended Jonathan, surprised at his own insight. Jonathan sat with those thoughts; he could not remember many prayers, except for a few from his childhood days. For the first time after decades in the wilderness, he recited them for Jasmin.

Traveling on the back of a horse wagon was a totally different experience for Jonathan and Dirum. On the way up with Mami, they somehow felt so connected. The closeness to Mami and the land they walked on gave them a sense of awareness. Now it was a matter of watching and observing.

Around dusk time, Salman stopped the wagon. "We will stop here for the night," he said as he stepped out and began to remove the harness from the horse.

Jonathan and Dirum were happy to find that Salman had stopped at a beautiful location right by a river. "You have picked a great place to camp," Dirum said.

"Yes, it is a nice spot. It has water and good grass, both important for our horse," responded Salman.

Jonathan seemed quite surprised by his response. Whereas he and Dirum were thinking about the location from their point of view, Salman seemed more concerned about the horse. How do you develop these instincts to think in such a selfless manner, Jonathan wondered?

After Salman had taken care of his horse, he set up a fire by the river. It was a glorious night. The sky was blue and a full moon graced the ceiling of earth. The river flowed downstream and the reflection of the moon on the water made it appear easy to reach. "Look at the moon," Jonathan said, "It is so clear and looks real, yet it is just a reflection. How do we know what we see with our eyes is not an illusion?"

Dirum thought about it for a while and said, "You are right, can we trust our eyes? Perhaps this whole thing is a dream. I remember a Sufi story; in it a dog comes to the river to drink some water. It sees its own reflection and runs away in fear because it thought there was another dog in the river."

"That is a good metaphor for us, we act and react because of illusions. Sometimes we act from fear, other times we are judgmental, the thought that our actions may be based on something unreal is disconcerting," added Jonathan, "Life is like that in the city."

"What do you mean?" Dirum asked.

"Our society has been moving ahead very rapidly, and the advances in science, technology and communications have pushed the limits of human capacity. It is taking its toll inflicting stress and distress within society. Being away from everything, it does become apparent. As they say, when you are in the woods you can't tell the trees from the forest. In the city you get caught up with everything. There is never any time to think, to question," said Jonathan as Dirum listened with great interest. Jonathan continued, "Not too long ago we built robots so that they could perform tasks we programmed. The idea was to have them act and follow our instructions precisely and to accomplish job functions. Today we have created technologies that are now turning us into robots. Click, point, send, auto archive, auto program, E-mail, E-trade, E-business, B2B. Our individuality is being drowned in a world where we are being programmed to act, behave and respond in an exact way, no matter which part of the world we live in. The world and our life in it has become clinical. We go to work in droves every morning, we complete our tasks and we come home. On the way home we pick up our homogenized, processed and prepacked foods, shrink-wrapped in chemicals and preservatives. Two minutes in the microwave and dinner is ready. The robot is fed and greased. Then we sit in front of the television. The mind is switched off so that we can be brainwashed. We are told what to buy, where to buy it, how to live and where to live, not to mention what to wear, the appropriate brands, and so all the values and rules of our consumer society are downloaded. Auto programming is done, so we sleep, ready for the next day. I know I was part of this. We are a robotic society conditioned to believe that bigger is better, more is a good thing, and that we must tirelessly pursue these ideals at any cost. As a member of the consumer society, we are told that it is our duty to strive to upgrade our homes, our cars, our vacations and our clothes in the name of a higher standard of living. Money, though, is never a barrier because there are enough lenders to accommodate all our dreams of luxury. So what do we do? We push ourselves because we are under some illusion that it will bring us that cherished idea of happiness and peace, a purpose in our life. Except it never does," Jonathan said.

"At what point do people stop to ask, what is real and what is not," Dirum asked despondently, familiar with Jonathan's description of society.

"The only time we stop to ask is when a crisis or some event shakes us out of our robotic state. Maybe during moments of sadness or when we have difficulties and problems we cannot solve by flinging our credit cards at them, like it happened to me," Jonathan responded. "When we look at this reflection of the moon, I can see how an illusion can actually become the reality for people, like it was for me," continued Jonathan after a moment of thought.

"Mami used to say that everything in life has a counterpart. I look at the moon and what he meant seems so clear," Dirum said.

Jonathan added, "Everything is making sense. Mami said that there is the physical and spiritual reality. Similarly, man has a lower and higher self, and that is exactly what we see. There is the moon in the river which is a reflection, yet high above is the reality."

Just then a cloud passed over the moon and its image in the river momentarily changed from white to blue. Jonathan and Dirum sat staring at each other and jumped up together screaming, "Express your higher self, that is the blue jewel of the Rainbow."

"Mami had said that so many times!" Jonathan exclaimed.

"It is funny, but you don't realize a moment sooner than you are supposed to," Dirum gasped with a tinge of excitement. "Now it fits together," he said.

"What?" questioned Jonathan.

"Do you remember how we wondered that if our

thoughts became our words, and these words in turn became our actions, then how could we control the quality of our thoughts?" asked Dirum.

"Yes, I do, because sometimes our thoughts really let us down. They can be jealous, greedy, envious, and vindictive. I mean, let's face it, sometimes we have shameful thoughts," Jonathan responded.

"Well, since all these thoughts are the product of the mind which is the lower self, the instruction of the blue jewel of the Rainbow is to operate out of your higher self," stated Dirum precisely.

"That's it, that's exactly what Mami told us, that operating from the lower self had turned us into Techno human beings," added Jonathan quite proudly.

Jonathan and Dirum sat in silence for quite some time. Both of them had come to cherish those moments of quiet contemplation.

Dirum broke the silence. "It is so simple, the higher self is the seat of the soul, that is where all our higher ethical and virtuous qualities like goodness, forgiveness, love and nobility reside. When we operate from there, we can transcend those debasing thoughts."

"It may be simple, but the trouble with man is that he cannot learn truths that are too complicated, and he forgets truths which are overly simple," Jonathan shrugged as he pulled up his sleeping bag.

As usual, Jonathan was the first one up in the morning. Salman put on the chai to which everyone was totally addicted. The river also gave them a good opportunity to bathe before they set off. Dirum and Jonathan sat at the back, whilst Salman drove the wagon. Around midday they heard a large rumbling in the distance. It seemed like thunder on the horizon. Salman seemed visibly nervous.

"What was that?" Dirum asked.

"That was a tremor. In the mountain ranges it happens a lot," he said. A few moments later the rumbling noise appeared again, this time it stayed drawing closer and closer. In an instance the earth beneath the wagon started to tremble and shake. Jonathan and Dirum looked at each other, wondering fearfully what they should do. Salman in the meantime was trying desperately to calm down the horse. The crashing of a nearby tree finally spooked the horse and he bolted. Salman hung on at the front, whilst Jonathan and Dirum were being thrown about at the back rather violently. As the horse galloped, fear seized Jonathan, whilst Dirum was too busy trying to avoid being thrown out of the wagon. The horse took a violent turn and the two side wheels of the carriage lifted, loosening Dirum's grip as he fell off the side. Jonathan watched helplessly as he heard Dirum's shout.

Finally Salman was able to reassure the horse, and the wagon halted. Shaking off his weak and rubbery legs Jonathan joined Salman to search for Dirum. The thought that something may have happened to him was troubling, as he ran frantically in search of his friend. About a mile away they found him sitting by the side of the path, and he was all right.

Jonathan was visibly relieved as Dirum spoke. "I am all right. I just have a few bruises. Are you both okay?"

"Yes, everyone is fine," Jonathan answered, still panting from his run up.

Salman tended to the horse. After removing the harness, he affectionately wiped him down. Jonathan and

Dirum, meanwhile, found a big tree under which to sit. "I thought I was going to die," Jonathan said.

"I did not have time to think of anything, seeing that I was just trying to hang on," Dirum added.

"What would you do today if you knew you were going to die tomorrow?" asked Jonathan, visibly shaken up and remembering Mami's words. "Everything in the physical world is temporary." Dirum pondered for a moment but before he could answer Jonathan continued, "I have traveled a lot—New York, Paris, London. I am good at it; I can pack my bag in an hour. I have it down pat; there is the toothpaste, toothbrush, and shaving things, PJs, day clothes, evening clothes, day shoes, evening shoes and travel documents. But as we were on that wagon out of control, it made me think. Mami had said that death is not the end, for there is life after each death in this perfect creation. So if I knew that I was going to die tomorrow, what would I pack for that journey?"

"Well, forget those suitcases you had packed to Paris for a start," Dirum responded spontaneously. "Yes, and you can also forget your home, cars and your other possessions," he added.

"My mutual funds too," offered Jonathan sarcastically.

"Mami used to say that doing worthwhile and noble things is an expression of the higher self, and that it uplifts the spirit. It then follows that whatever good we do, we can take with us," Dirum said confidently. "I was told a story a long time ago and the metaphors in it left a deep impression on me. It went like this:

"Once upon a time there was a rich merchant who had four wives. He loved the fourth wife the most and adorned her with rich robes and treated her to delicacies.

120

He took great care of her and gave her nothing but the best.

He also loved the third wife very much. He was very proud of her and always wanted to show her off to his friends. However, the merchant was always in great fear that she might run away with some other man.

He loved his second wife, too, and she would always help him out and tide him through difficult times.

Now, the merchant's first wife was a very loyal partner and had made great contributions in maintaining his wealth and business as well as taking care of the household. However, the merchant did not love the first wife, and although she loved him deeply, he hardly took notice of her.

One day, the merchant fell ill. Before long, he knew that he was going to die soon. He thought of his luxurious life and told himself, 'Now I have four wives with me. But when I die, I'll be alone. How lonely I'll be!'

Thus, he asked the fourth wife, 'I loved you most, endowed you with the finest clothing and showered great care over you. Now that I'm dying, will you follow me and keep me company?'

'No,' replied the fourth wife, and she walked away without another word. The answer cut like a sharp knife into the merchant's heart.

The sad merchant then asked the third wife, 'I have loved you so much for all my life. Now that I'm dying, will you follow me and keep me company?'

'No,' replied the third wife. 'Life is so good over here! I'm going to remarry when you die!' The merchant's heart sank and turned cold.

He then asked the second wife. 'I always turned to you for help and you've always helped me out. Now I need your help again. When I die, will you follow me and keep me company?'

'I am sorry. I can't help you this time!' replied the second wife. 'At the very most, I can only send you to your grave.'

The answer came like a bolt of lightening and the merchant was devastated.

Then a voice called out. 'I'll leave with you. I'll follow you no matter where you go.'

The merchant looked up and there was his first wife. She was so skinny, almost like she suffered from malnutrition.

Greatly grieved, the merchant said, 'I should have taken much better care of you while I could have!'"

"Actually, we all have four wives in our lives," Dirum continued. "The fourth wife is our body. No matter how much time and effort we lavish in making it look good, it'll leave us when we die. Our third wife? Our possessions, status and wealth. When we die, they all go to others. The second wife is our family and friends. No matter how much they had been there for us when we're alive, the furthest they can stay by us is up to the grave. The first wife is in fact our soul, often neglected in our pursuit of material wealth and sensual pleasure. Guess what? It is actually the only thing that follows us wherever we go. Perhaps it's a good idea to cultivate and strengthen it now rather than to wait until we're on our deathbed to lament."

"You are right, we are like the ravens attracted by the glitter of the material life. In the process, we ignore the most important aspect of our being, the spirit within. As Mami had said, life was like a string on a bow. Tighten it too much and it would snap. Keep it too loose and the arrow will not fly. The key to happiness was to avoid the extremes and find the balance. We need to nurture both the physical and spiritual in order to reach the harmonious level of existence. Someone once told me that good deeds are the only things that nourish the spirit. The one thing that does remain after physical death is the soul and our deeds are attached to it," said Jonathan as he began to embrace this wisdom.

They sat and observed some tadpoles in a small puddle of water, acknowledging that the death of the tadpole will be the birth of the frog.

"My father used to tell me a story," Dirum said, and he recounted his dad's words in a tale.

"A mystic once asked a rich man what he loved most, his riches and possessions or the sins he committed.

The rich man said, 'My wealth and possessions, of course.'

The mystic responded by saying, 'You lie, you love sin more.' 'Why?' asked the rich man, who did not understand.

'Well,' replied the mystic, 'because you will leave behind your riches, and you will take your sins with you.'

Then he advised the rich man to spend a part of his wealth on the needy. This way he would be taking it with him."

"A fitting metaphor, that's what Mami would have said," Jonathan responded. How come you know so many stories that are loaded with meanings and metaphors?"

"Well, they are Sufi stories. Sufi's are taught wisdom through the metaphors, similes and allegories contained in these profound stories," Dirum answered.

"What is a Sufi?" asked Jonathan.

"Sufism is an esoteric path for those who seek the knowledge and experience of the universal soul. It is a purpose that takes a central and pivotal role in their physical life," Dirum answered precisely before changing the subject. "You miss Mami, don't you?" Dirum asked, looking deep into Jonathan's eyes.

"Yes I do," replied Jonathan with his lost dog expression.

"Well, you should not," Dirum said.

"Why?" Jonathan asked, surprised.

"Because I see him with you. There is a lot of Mami in many things you say," he answered sincerely. That made Jonathan feel good and he reminisced about him. Dirum interrupted his thoughts. "Did you open that gift you received from the villagers?" asked Dirum.

"No, I totally forgot," Jonathan said.

"Me, too," Dirum said as he walked to the wagon to find them. Dirum returned shortly with two identical packages and handed one over to Jonathan. Inside the box was a book with a hardbound cover. It was strikingly beautiful—a black cover with bright splashes of violet spreading out.

"It's a Rumi," Dirum said excitedly. Jonathan looked up, though the gift was obviously very beautiful, he was not familiar with the author. "Rumi is one of the greatest poets ever. In these parts of the world he is a legend. The West is only just beginning to discover his work," Dirum exclaimed, noticing Jonathan's blank face.

"Tell me about him." Jonathan began flipping the pages.

"His work is profound and spiritual, it is simple yet so complex, and it has allegories and metaphors that teach us important lessons about ourselves," Dirum answered.

Poetry was Dirum's favorite pastime; he had learnt much about life reading the works of Omar Khayyam, Rumi and other poets. Jonathan's eyes flashed as he digested Dirum's words. "It is the violet of the rainbow, life is a lesson," he shouted. "Dirum, you have done it again, you and Rumi have conspired to bring me the violet jewel of the Rainbow. Everything that happens in life is a lesson from which we can grow," said Jonathan, unable to sit with excitement.

"You've got it, Jonathan, life is continually prodding and pushing us, like the wind, sometimes it's in our back aiding us, at other times it's in our face causing us discomfort, but in every case it is talking, communicating and teaching us. We need to draw the lesson. Just like Rumi's book. Life's circumstances are filled with metaphors," Dirum concluded enthusiastically.

"Mami once told me a story," Jonathan began, remembering his words on this subject. "There was a lamp and in it was water. On top of the water lay oil. The wick reached into the oil and burnt brightly. One day the water complained to the oil, 'I am water; I am the most precious thing in creation. Without me all life would perish. So I am the one who should be above, but instead you are above, and I am below.' The oil responded sympathetically. 'I can understand your pain, but I was amongst the black tar in the ground. They dug me up with excavators, they broke me and crushed me, and then I was put on conveyor belts where I was put through a temperature hotter than the sun. Through this pain and struggle I was purified and became oil only after suffering all that. This is why I am above you.'"

"That is a typical Mami story, and it's loaded," Dirum

said. "Life does push us to learn and grow. Good times may be easier lessons, but hard times develop strong spirits."

"Yes, but only if we have learnt a lesson in every circumstance," added Jonathan thoughtfully.

Chapter 11

*"The journey to union was only a matter of two steps;
because of thy noose I have remained 60 years on the way."*[1]

Salman shouted from a distance, "Let's go." He had calmed the horse and given him time to relax in the meadow. Jonathan and Dirum returned with their books, as Salman was putting the final harness around the horse. The small earthquake had slowed them down. However, they still hoped to be in Gilgit that night.

Noticing Jonathan dig into the book, Dirum said, "You have a lot in common with Rumi."

"In what way?" Jonathan asked.

"He too went through a profound transformation in his life, just like you have," answered Dirum.

Jonathan reflected on everything that happened and how it had given him a new perspective. "It is not that I have changed, it is just that I have found myself," he said as he wished Crystal could be with him now. "Tell me about Rumi and what happened in his life."

Dirum sat up and told the tale of Rumi's life. "Rumi was a very learned scholar. He was known to be one the brightest of all the scholars of his time. He could quote theories and explain the words from the holy texts very eloquently. One day he met an enigmatic mystic by the name of Shamsh Tabriz. In his usual manner Rumi was very arrogant and sure about himself and his knowledge. Shamsh Tabriz told Rumi that his knowledge was useless because it was all learnt, but Rumi articulated a great rebuttal to the mystic's criticism. So one day when they were having a discussion by the lake, Shamsh Tabriz threw all of Rumis's important books and manuscripts into the water. Rumi was incensed and terribly angry.

Shamsh Tabriz asked Rumi, 'Now that all your books are in the water, where is your knowledge?' That stopped Rumi in his tracks, it totally stumped him. What was his knowledge without the books, he thought. He spent days thinking about it. One day Shamsh Tabriz visited him and brought him his books. Rumi was further shocked. How could Shamsh have retrieved all those damaged books and returned them? Shamsh told Rumi that his knowledge was of this world, all of it learnt. Yet there was a higher knowledge called wisdom. It was at this time that the transformation of Rumi begun. He threw away all his books and became a disciple of Shamsh Tabriz to understand the higher knowledge of wisdom. This book by Rumi was written later in his life after his metamorphosis."

"That is so interesting," Jonathan said.

"If you read the poems you will notice not only his laments and experiences, but it also becomes apparent that Rumi had achieved a high level of enlightenment," clarified Dirum as he recited a verse from the book.

When at the hour of death that pure draught is separated
from the bodily clod by dying,
thou quickly buriest that which remains,
since it had been made such an ugly thing by that separation.
When the spirit displays its beauty without this carcass,
I cannot express the loveliness of the union.

"You mean that he had reached a point where he lived in harmony with the flow of energy from the universal soul?" Jonathan asked, taken aback by the depth of the words.

"Yes, after all we are our worst enemies. The only thing that stops us achieving exalted destinies is ourselves," Dirum answered.

"Our lower self," Jonathan added, clarifying his point while continuing to ponder Rumi's insightful verse.

The afternoon went slowly, both Dirum and Jonathan remained rather quiet and introspective. The journey's end was appearing and a somber feeling of sadness permeated the rumbling wagon. Around dusk they stopped near a settlement. Salman needed to rest the horse a while, and Dirum and Jonathan took the opportunity to wander about and stretch their legs. They found a nice spot overlooking the valley. Some of the workers were still busily working the fields.

"What are they working at?" asked Jonathan gazing at the workers in the valley below and not recognizing the crop.

"Those are indigofera plants; you can tell from the color. The bluish shade from the indigo," Dirum answered.

"What do they do with the crop?" Jonathan inquired, never having heard of an indigofera plant.

"The indigofera plant is used in part as a herbal supplement. However, the more important and common use of it is that they make the indigo dye from it," he answered.

"How come I have not seen much of this dye around during our travels?"

"Well, actually they export the indigo dye to the western world including Canada and the U.S.A. The dye is then used in fabrics, like the jeans you are wearing," answered Dirum, staring at his faded denims.

Jonathan thought about it for some time and said, "Isn't it odd that everything in life seems to follow its own rhythm. Like Mami said, nature is perfectly balanced. I mean even the people we have met seem to have their own natural plan. Just look at that plant, it becomes an indigo dye, goes to Canada, yet here I am wearing it, allowing it to return to its own origin."

Dirum just looked at Jonathan in amazement, who spontaneously returned the look. "It's found us." They screamed together, "It's indigo, the last jewel of the Rainbow."

"Indigo is the last jewel of the Rainbow. Everyone has to discover their own plan," Jonathan said, as he jumped on Dirum in a friendly tussle.

"There is a definitive flow within our creation. Why does a bird sing, a lion roar or a snake hiss? There is a plan for everything, including us," Dirum exclaimed, dusting his trousers.

"That's right, and anything which is at odds to the plan will feel the pain of exclusion. So we must discover our own plan or mission, only then can we get in sync with the natural flow," Jonathan cautioned as he remembered a story. "Mami had told me this story. At that time I did not quite get it. There was a man who lived by a beautiful river. It flowed serenely past his house. One day he decided to build a bigger home. So he embarked on his mission breaking down the old house to build a new one. Without realizing it, the debris from the construction was falling into the river, slowly stifling the water's flow. The river was getting blocked and it changed directions as they often do. Soon it no longer went past his house, and he wondered why. He did not realize that the problems were his own doing and created over a period of time. Now he had lost the supply of water that flowed by his house."

"It makes sense because often we have created obstacles in our own life accidentally. If we are involved in things, which are not part of our plan, we are stifling our flow. As a result we may feel unhappy or depressed. By adapting and realigning ourselves we can create a positive change in our lives. This can only be done by discovering our own mission," Dirum concluded.

"It is true that sometimes we find out for ourselves that we are on the wrong path and so we make changes in our life; other times we are at such odds that life forces a change upon us. Sooner or later though, it is bound to happen. One can only swim against the tide for so long. Then something drastic happens and you get the proverbial wake-up call," Jonathan confirmed as he thought about his own situation. "In hindsight, I did not have a clue. I kept snapping at life, rebelling and defying it. One day it just snapped back and I was back flowing with the tide," Jonathan said, feeling rather sorry for himself.

"Sometimes life forces bad medicine into our lives to cure us back on the right track," added Dirum rather sympathetically.

"Now I understand what Cat Stevens did," Jonathan said.

"Who is Cat Stevens?"

"He was a truly gifted artist, a singer and song writer. He was extremely famous and his songs were very meaningful, like poems. I used to get joy out of listening to him.

131

One day at the top of his fame, and out of the blue, he quit singing and writing. He gave everything up, to follow his own mission in life. I could never understand, why? But now I do. He discovered his own plan and had the courage to change his direction despite the perceived worldly cost." Jonathan withdrew into himself as one of his songs played in his mind. He is so right he thought. Life is indeed just like a maze of doors and they always seem to open the side we are on. The harder we try, the more we end up right back where we started from.

Dirum's words interrupted Jonathan. "Isn't it simple, that everyone has a personal plan, yet no one can say if one person's mission is worth more or less than someone else's. You have an old man pick indigofera plants, a woman who may care for her elderly parents, an astronaut may go to the moon, or the person who is elected as the president of a nation: Each has a plan that is equally important."

"That's right, comparisons and judgments are odious. As Mami used to say, there is a hierarchy with humans and no one knows who is more illuminated. Yet our personal mission in life is always planned to help us grow. So we must embrace it and flow with it," Jonathan added, as he thought about the time Crystal quit her high-paying job to stay home with the children.

Jonathan's emotions had soared effervescently at the discovery of the final jewel. It represented the culmination of a long and arduous journey. However as he sat silently thinking deeply about all that had happened a more somber mood engulfed him. A cold shiver ran up his spine as the realization dawned on him that he had in his possession the very blueprints that would bring mankind happiness, harmony and success. These were the seven jewels of the rainbow, the total approach to balanced living. This prize would have satisfied most people. Not so with Jonathan who felt himself sinking into a deep void. It was during these intense contemplative moments that he remembered Mami's words. "Happiness and success are prisons too! Only when the subject merges with the object is there true liberation." Jonathan meditated on those words for quite some time before concluding that though happiness and success should have been enough, he yearned for more and upon this he continued to agonize.

Chapter 12

*"O fierie wind, before thee I am but straw:
how can I know where I shall fall."*[1]

*I*t was midnight and they were still some two hours from
Gilgit. The accident had slowed them but they had
made up some of the time. Jonathan was engrossed in his
thought; the seven jewels of the Rainbow, those ancient
and sacred blueprints for achieving happiness, harmony
and success were in his hands, yet something deep within
his spirit told him to go beyond. He had come to the
conclusion that the one true thing he wished for was the
wisdom to experience that oneness with the universal
soul. This picture consumed him. Slowly it dawned on
him that it was indeed the pinnacle to which man could
aspire. Jonathan realized that worldly status, wealth and
possessions were incomparable, just like the largest tree
held against the backdrop of Mount Everest.

The craving of this experience was painful, and finally
he knew the meaning of Sufism Dirum had tried so hard
to explain. It was an esoteric path that culminated in the
direct experience of the eternal, the universal soul.
Jonathan now understood why Dirum had avoided an
explanation of Sufism. Academic knowledge of it made us
helpless in distinguishing between the external symbols
and the essence. It could only be understood by going
beyond rational thought. Jonathan willingly surrendered
knowing full well that this path offered no instant solu-
tions. The call to scale the heights was strong, but it was a

journey that demanded struggle, patience and sacrifice. He remembered that the first step was to find the seven jewels of the Rainbow, and just as Mami had said, he never had to reach out, they had found him.

The green jewel was meditation. Since the journey to truth and enlightenment was an inward one, it followed that for those seeking that which was within, there was just one solitary path. Meditation was the only conceivable route to reach inwards into the depth of our being.

The red jewel was to rid ourselves of pride, for it gave us an illusion of our own self worth. Having an inflated image of ourselves automatically puts us at odds with our own natural flow in life. Furthermore, it engineers arrogance and subdues humility, which is a necessary disposition for enlightenment.

The orange of the jewel tells us not to be judgmental, because we live in an illusionary world. Man's ideas and perceptions are a product of his upbringing and previous experiences. Every person carries conditioning and prejudices from the past. Being judgmental sinks us into our lower self. Such expressions harm us because they are born of deception.

The yellow jewel told us to be generous, because it was a noble human expression. It represents actions and choices that no other created thing on earth is endowed with. No living being has the instinctive ability to be kind, charitable, helpful, compassionate, caring and giving. This lofty action of selflessness is a choice granted only human beings. Service to others, especially to the old, sick, orphans, the weak and the poor is, without question, life's great calling.

The blue jewel calls us to express our higher self in every situation, because this raises us up from the physical level to the spiritual one. Since the only element in life that we can control is our response, the blue jewel expects our responses to emerge from our higher self. Jealousy, envy, malicious gossip, lust, anger, vindictiveness, bitterness, hatred are debasing qualities which bring man to the same level as that of the animals. These expressions are predominant in their world. However, forgiveness, tolerance, patience, humility, selflessness, honesty, righteousness and such are qualities that raise man above the profane world of time and space.

The violet jewel was about learning a lesson in every circumstance. Every human goes through his or her own personal seasons, just like in nature. Good and bad times in life can be equated with summer and winter. It is not the seasons that matter but what we experience from them. Life provides infinite opportunities for us to learn from every situation, to find the wisdom in every incident and to grow from every season. Lessons to be learnt are often not obvious and they have to be sought.

The indigo jewel of the rainbow extols us to discover our own plan and mission, so that we are not at odds with the energy of the universal soul. Everyone has a personal plan, which is unique. Happiness and purpose are feelings that are experienced when each one is in their own missions. Some have large missions; others have lots of smaller ones. Each should seek their own plan and avoid comparison.

Jonathan understood the merits and importance of each jewel of the Rainbow, recognizing the wisdom in each, yet he could still not see how they could help him scale the highest peak of all. That of the direct experience of the universal soul, the source of all things. In his mind he continued re-living all the moments with Mami. Somewhere in that valuable time was the missing piece.

All along, the image of Mami standing with tears in his eyes, up against the glory of the rainbow was predominant. The rainbow had everything to do with his quest. Yet Jonathan had also come to understand that wisdom was completely unlike knowledge. Learnt knowledge was something man controls. He can act and respond in achieving that which he seeks purely out of the outcome of his effort and labor. Just like reaching out to take something, it was an idea that was in his power. Wisdom was a different thing altogether. It is rarely attained by effort or hard work. It cannot be taken or reached for, like Rumi, when he craved wisdom enough, he found the courage to let go of everything he had learnt. For wisdom is a grace, which is offered, not taken. Jonathan realized that he was also helpless to reach and take; he had never learnt this at Harvard.

Jonathan recalled that day by the fireside.

"Mami, tell me about the universal soul."

"It is above all, yet it is closer to us than our jugular vein. Its light illuminates creation at all times, alas, mankind is like bats, blind to it. Whilst humanity is preoccupied in calculating how many seeds there are in every apple, only the universal soul can tell how many apples there are in every seed. It has a perfect plan for every seed, for every grain of sand, for every living thing, yet some men choose to ignore the ocean on account of the waves," Mami had answered sincerely. "The seeds of that fruit are within you," Mami had said allegorically. What did he mean by the seeds of that fruit are within me, and how does the Rainbow fit into this equation. I wish the Rainbow could talk, thought Jonathan, as the wagon rolled into the outskirts of Gilgit.

Dirum lay fast asleep. Jonathan stared up into the dark sky and remembered something Mami had said. "When I was young, I knew everything. Now I know nothing, wisdom is the discovery of our own ignorance."

Chapter 13

"When the barrier in front and barrier behind are removed, the eye penetrates and reads the tablet of the unseen."[1]

*D*irum called out, "Wake up Jonathan! Wake up!" Jonathan crawled out of bed, glanced at his wrist and demanded, "What is the time?"

"It is ten in the morning," said Dirum. "This has to be a record, I actually awoke before you," Dirum teased.

"Well I was up late in the wagon because a certain someone was snoring so loud, I couldn't sleep," Jonathan teased back.

Jonathan was rather quiet as he changed into some clothes. There seemed to be an eerie feeling, a void of sorts that created a distance between Dirum and Jonathan. The thought that this was the end did not escape either of them. The small talk was painful for it hid the tremendous love and respect they had for each other. They knew deep down that they lived in different worlds, yet fate had conspired to bring them together for a time and in that they grew.

"You will be glad to know that the border between India and Pakistan is now open," Dirum stated.

"Oh, so they figured out that they are not going to bomb each other," Jonathan said with a tinge of sarcasm.

"I will be leaving for Bombay this evening. What about you?" Dirum asked.

"My return trip to Toronto goes from Delhi in two days time so, I was thinking that if I went to Delhi this evening it will give me the opportunity to visit the Taj Mahal," Jonathan replied.

"That is really a good idea. The Taj Mahal is in Agra, which is close to Delhi. There is an express train that can take you there and back. I think you really will get a lot from that trip," Dirum said, supporting the idea.

"Dirum, you know there are still some loose ends. I feel I have come so far, and together we have discovered truths, yet something is missing," Jonathan said rather sadly.

"I know, and it is bothering me, too, but we have learnt that this is not a treasure hunt, wisdom invariably finds you in its own time. It's not in our hands, as Mami once said, 'you can't push on a string. Despite the urge to reach and take, the higher self calls for surrender;' alas it will appear when it does. All we can do is continue to yearn for it," responded Dirum philosophically as he reminisced of a conversation with Mami. "Sometimes I feel so helpless, I am pulled apart by the turmoil and problems in my physical life on the one hand and the yearning for calm by my innerself on the other." Dirum had questioned Mami, drawing on his personal experiences. "Is the soil not pained and troubled when the farm toils the land? Yet a bountiful harvest is the eventual outcome. My friend, as the soil trusted the farmer, so too, must we trust life." Mami had answered sympathetically.

"Why don't you come to Delhi with me? You can show me the Taj Mahal. Not the one I see in the brochure, but the one that's in your heart. It would mean so much to me," Jonathan asked, hoping Dirum would say yes.

Dirum's face lit up. "I would love to do that."

Dirum and Jonathan boarded the plane later that afternoon, having made the changes to their travel itineraries.

It was a comfortable flight; however, their discomfort in crowded places was noticeable. Having spent so much time in open spaces with few people and little noise, it took them a while to get used to the hustle and bustle prevalent in the cities.

They arrived in Delhi at night and took a cab to the center. Dirum was quite familiar with the city and had already picked out the hotel. No sooner had they left the airport, and the poverty became very apparent. The sidewalks were either bustling in the commercial activities of street vendors, or they were sleeping spots claimed by the innumerable homeless.

Jonathan was up bright and early the next morning. By the time Dirum awoke, the chai had already been ordered. They planned to leave very early in the morning. Dirum had wished to visit the Taj Mahal during a time when the tourist activity was at its lowest. They were in Delhi central station in time to catch the express to Agra, a small town in the vicinity of the Taj Mahal. The train left the station and Jonathan watched with tremendous interest at the sight of India waking.

There were many rivers along the way, Jonathan observed. A man rowing a boat made Jonathan remember a conversation with Mami. "Do you remember when we stopped briefly at the river with Mami?" Jonathan asked, distracting Dirum from a magazine he had picked up.

"Yes; this was after we crossed that small summit," Dirum answered.

"I was sitting with him just looking out at the fast flow of the river. Do you remember seeing someone in a row boat?" Jonathan asked.

"No, I don't recall anyone in a boat."

143

"For some time the man in the boat was trying to row upstream. You could tell sitting on the side that sooner or later he would run out of energy. For sure the river was not going to change its flow. Mami said to me that life is like that river. It has a certain flow. It is fluid and constantly moving in a certain predetermined direction. When we do things which are in opposition to that flow, sooner or later it ends in some consequence. If we can only live our lives in that flow, we can avoid half of the stress and pain we encounter. As an observer I could see the hopeless situation of the boat's man and could predict the eventual outcome," Jonathan said.

"That is just the way it is. Even when we flow with the river there are hurdles to cross, but then to row upstream we are simply increasing the obstacles. Yet unlike the rower in the boat, the key is to be aware of the flow within our lives in the first place and to walk in that rhythm rather than against it," Dirum pronounced.

Jonathan pulled out the colored stones of the rainbow and placed them on the table between them. "I think that these jewels of the Rainbow we discovered can help us become aware of our personal rhythm," said Jonathan.

"How so?"

"Mami had said that everything returns to its origin. Our physical body returns to its source, the earth. Our spiritual self returns to the universal soul. The flow of life Mami was referring to was not our physical one, right?" Jonathan asked, looking for confirmation.

"That's right, our spiritual existence has dominion, and that's the one that truly matters," Dirum answered.

"Mami had said that we must get into the flow of the energy of the universal soul. There is no way that we can perceive this with our five senses, seeing, touching, hearing, smelling and tasting, because these cannot help us," said Jonathan.

"So how do we figure out if we are in the right flow?"

"Mami had started and ended the day with meditation. Meditation is what he used to sense if he was in the right flow," Jonathan said confidently.

"You are right, meditation is a spiritual tool. It enables us to connect within ourselves. We strengthen that connection and we discover the universal pulse," added Dirum rather enthusiastically placing his magazine away and picking up the green stone. "Each one of these colors of the Rainbow are precious jewels, because they somehow point us towards our true calling. Collectively they raise us up to what Mami called 'the true status of Humanity.'"

"How do the difficulties people face in their lives fit into this scheme of things? Sickness, disease, things just not working out, you know, events which we generally do not control," Jonathan asked as he watched a broken car on the side of the road.

"Some of these problems are a consequence of our own doing. If we are at odds with the flow, life will conspire to change directions. We may feel pain or experience problems on the physical level as a result, but it is the inevitable consequence of the laws of the physical life in which we operate," Dirum said.

"Yes, but you could be in the right flow and still experience these difficulties," said Jonathan.

"That's right, other times these circumstances develop by their own accord, but these are the things which move us forward. Remember, as the movement of the oceans in the physical plain is created by the pull of the gravity, similarly, our pull in the right direction on the spiritual plain happens with growing and changing," Dirum answered.

"I get it, we need circumstances that will change us. That is why the indigo jewel asks us to learn a lesson in every circumstance, and that's how we grow," beamed Jonathan as he started to smile to himself.

"Why are you smiling?" Dirum asked.

"I was just thinking about this little nursery rhyme I used to sing to my daughter, Jasmin, about a spider who kept climbing up the water pipe. Each time the water came and washed him back down. It is so ironic people are like that, too, because things happen to us, but we just don't get it. We never learn the lesson," Jonathan concluded.

"A fitting metaphor, Mami would say," said Dirum with a smile.

Chapter 14

"He opened the inward eye and gazed on the ideal form
of that which he had only read in books."[1]

*T*he train sped through the countryside, and the little towns that occasionally passed by showed the raw simplicity of the way hundreds of millions of people lived. The standard of living, if compared to Western yardsticks, would demonstrate abject poverty. Yet, men, women and children went about their business following their own plan. The rumbling of the train navigating a corner shook the table, rolling the colored stones to one side, catching Dirum and Jonathan's eyes.

"Mami used to say that there is an exoteric and esoteric aspect to everything, an inner and outer manifestation in all things. Therefore this rainbow that hides so much within itself, visibly it is a splendor, yet beyond its outer beauty, hidden deep within itself was a greater treasure. Help me understand the Rainbow, Dirum," Jonathan asked.

"Contemplation and actions," Dirum answered.

"I don't understand," Jonathan confessed.

"Think back when Mami told us that everything we see in the perceptible world is a reflection of an inner reality. There are two dimensions: one, which is visible, and its counterpart, that is not. The rainbow we see is as the body of man, but the essence is nobler," Dirum said as he picked the colored stones of the Rainbow. Slowly Dirum separated them into two groups. He put the red, orange and yellow on one side and the blue, green, violet and indigo on the other side. "These four colors of the rainbow, blue, green, violet and indigo represent the inner esoteric dimension of the rainbow. These three, red, orange and yellow are its visible and exoteric counterpart," explained Dirum.

"It is falling into place," said Jonathan rather introspectively. "The four inner colors represent contemplation. It is the foundation of the rainbow. They are like wings that can be spread enabling us to soar. Meditation, expressing your higher self, seeing life as a lesson and discovering your plan, these are the ethos.

"The three outer colors represent action. It is a visible manifestation. They represent the anchors that bind us to the world of the profane. By subduing pride, being non-judgmental and expressing generosity, we are releasing these anchors. Dirum, that's what Mami was saying, the Rainbow is a metaphor for man. It is everything we can be and should be."

Dirum picked up the colored stones and put them in the pouch. "Some people see themselves as the Rainbow. That's what Mami said. Now I know what he meant," Dirum exclaimed.

"Yes, and those tears spoke volumes because that morning, Mami was the Rainbow. This is what we all aspire to be," Jonathan said, evoking those sentiments he had experienced when he had felt Mami's hand on his shoulder.

Dirum and Jonathan slipped into reflection. Neither would ever see the Rainbow in the same way again. It had become a metaphor that symbolized the highest potential of man, a splendor within creation with an exalted destiny. The train slowed down suddenly jolting them out of their realization. As the train rolled to a halt in Agra, Dirum and Jonathan's mood had changed. It was still quite early and hailing a cab was easy. The taxis were always easy to find, convenient and cost very little. A cab could be kept a whole day for fewer than ten dollars.

Dirum was familiar with Agra, whilst Jonathan observed everything intently. The cab left the station bound for the Taj Mahal.

"Tell me about the Taj Mahal," Jonathan said.

"It is a monument of love; it's a symbol of the power of eternal love," said Dirum. "It was built by the fifth Mogul emperor Shah Jahan in 1631, in the memory of his wife Mumtaz Mahal, a Muslim Persian princess. It took twenty-two years to build, twenty-two thousand people worked on it, and a fleet of one thousand elephants were used to transport the marble. An Iranian architect, Isad Usa, designed it. It is without question beautiful and a work of art, but it is much more than that. Sir Edwin Arnold, the English poet wrote,

Not a piece of architecture,
As other buildings are,
But the proud passions of an emperor's love
written in living stone.

Although it is a sight to behold, its real beauty is the energy you feel, and it is alive with wonder."

"What kind of energy is it?" Jonathan asked.

"It's hard to explain; it is a feeling of enduring love. Timelessness. Rabindranth Tagore a poet described it better as 'a teardrop on the cheek of time,'" answered Dirum slowly.

Chapter 15

"Listen to the reed how it tells a tale, complaining of separations.
Saying, 'Ever since I was parted from the reed-bed,
my lament hath caused man and women to moan.'"[1]

The cab pulled up outside the expansive grounds. It was a long walk to the main entrance, and Jonathan strode briskly next to Dirum, his heart beating excitedly in anticipation. As the two men approached the main gate, they simultaneously noticed that the appearance of the gate resembled a veil on a woman's face. When they entered the large door, they were finally able to glimpse the Taj Mahal in the distance, and it seemed like the veil had been lifted to reveal the beauty. The Taj Mahal stood majestically before them, appearing to be afloat on the bank of the Yamuna River.

Jonathan and Dirum continued to walk toward it, passing through the immense courtyards. The subdued sunlight made the crown palace rather pinkish. The monument seemed like a mirage thought Jonathan because it seemed so surreal. The Taj Mahal emanated an aura that was indescribable. A sense of history filled the air, as did the purity of what one man could feel for a woman and the power of that emotion. The magnificent masterpiece was the artwork of what love could unleash.

"I am so glad I came. Truly I feel humbled in its presence," Jonathan said after a long silence that had all but magnetized his thoughts.

"Let us move away from it a little and sit, since it can be felt only when we are away from the clatter of visitors," Dirum suggested.

The two friends walked to one side away from the movement of tourists and found a comfortable spot to sit and etch the marvel into their mind. It was still the early part of the morning and the mist was beginning to lift. To their amazement, a Rainbow emerged, completing what seemed to be a sign for everything Dirum and Jonathan had searched for.

The highest potential of man and the loftiest status it could aspire to, symbolized by the Rainbow, had come face to face with man's noblest and purest of all expression, Love. Few words were spoken as instinctively Jonathan and Dirum faded into contemplation, captivated by its majesty.

As the sun moved past noon into late afternoon, the Taj Mahal looked milky white. Later when the sun set, the moon cleaved out from under, and at that time a golden glow emanated from the crown palace. It was the Jewels sparkling in the moonlight. Dirum and Jonathan emerged from their meditation. The dried tracks of tears on their cheeks gleamed occasionally as the moon stood in awe. Slowly they turned their faces and looked at one another. Their expression told of their ecstatic experience of the universal soul.

"It happened, I felt the energy of the universal soul," spoke Jonathan in total disbelief.

"Me too, in a split second, I experienced its certainty," Dirum said unable to think or talk with any clarity.

"What happened? Though no words were spoken, I was enlightened and have the answers of everything

I sought within me," Jonathan said solemnly.

Dirum looked up and asked, "Have you heard of Hafez, the Persian poet?"

Jonathan shook his head. "No."

Dirum continued, "Well, his words can give you solace and meaning better then I can." Then Dirum recited the poet's words.

When you have become headless and footless
in any way of the sustainer,
You will be transformed into his light from head to foot.

Jonathan reflected upon the poet's words. Indeed he had allowed himself to be consumed and in the process the subject merged with the object momentarily. "Everything, my life, my quest, my questions seem so insignificant in the face of this experience," reflected Jonathan, rather perplexed and overcome.

"That is the inevitable consequence of the intimate union with the supreme. A candle no matter how bright is pale and insignificant when put against the radiance of the sun," responded Dirum assuring himself and his companion.

They caught the evening express train from Agra to Delhi as planned. However, neither had counted on how the day would turn out. Silence permeated their thoughts as both recalled again and again their epiphanic experience. It was dark outside as the train traveled through the countryside. The occasional light from the burning wood fire brought back memories of their journey with Mami.

"I wonder where he is?" Jonathan wondered aloud, not really expecting a definitive response.

"Some people come into our lives and quickly go. Some stay for a while and leave footprints in our hearts and we are never the same again," Dirum answered with the look of a changed man.

"I am overcome. An odd unexplainable feeling engulfs me. For some reason, the questions I had are no longer puzzles; rather, they are certainties within me," confessed Jonathan.

"As we let go, this wisdom emerges in illumination of its own accord. That is the language of the universal soul. Though it is something given and not something reached for, in our submission is our transcendence," added Dirum thoughtfully.

Jonathan sat there putting the whole puzzle together in his own mind. The impetus and inspiration came from within him. He saw the image of Mami and remembered asking him how he could experience the energy of the universal soul. Find the precious seeds, plant them and be sure to nourish them, was his answer.

Mami started my journey by forcing me to ask the most important question of all. Who am I? Naively I believed that there was someone who would tell me. The baggage of my upbringing made me think that wealth and other resources could help me find the answer to this question. Instead this became a quest during which I discovered that the real me was as unique as the Rainbow. Furthermore I could only know the real me by first becoming enlightened. This is the case for every human being. I soon learnt that becoming enlightened was not something one could simply reach for. Reaching and taking was the domain of the physical realm. Mami became a teacher who taught us the laws of the spiritual domain.

Just like a radio that never catches your favorite station until it is tuned, Jonathan reflected how Mami's invisible role moved him into harmony with the Universal soul. Ultimately this was necessary to experience the real self. The process was slow; patience and labor were keys in this path. However, throughout everything, Mami remained the transcendent guide as he does today. He could have just told me, thought Jonathan, yet he knew that answers are meaningless. Libraries and bookstores are filled with treasure after treasure explaining the meaning of life and how to achieve happiness. They have no relevance without a personal search. Only this leads to realization. It is not the destination, but the journey, which creates enlightenment. The only matter of consequence is to ask, are we on the right journey or are we like a hamster in a wheel eluding ourselves into believing that what we seek is just around the corner. Mami made me realize that meditation had a way of keeping us on the right rhythm and flow, confirmed Jonathan to himself:

First he told me of the rainbow, and I admired its splendor. Then he asked me to find the essence of it. Without effort the seven colors of the rainbow found me. Mami than helped me understand that the rainbow was a metaphor for everything I could be, yet I was still missing a link. The old lady in the store told me of the importance of seeds but its meaning eluded me. Mami reminded me of the precious seeds and somehow I was still blind to it. Finally he opened my eyes and made me realize that the seven colors of the rainbow were precious because they were the seeds. Those seeds have to be planted within us. I did this. Finally the story the old lady had told me at Rabbya's store in Gilgit started to make sense. Happiness and success weren't items I could acquire; rather they were life's greatest gift surrendered to those who planted the seven jewels of the rainbow into their own lives. As I discovered each jewel, I practiced its ethos. I began to meditate about my own essence, which set me off on the journey of my own discovery. I tried at all times and in all situations, no matter how difficult, to express my higher self and to learn the wisdom in the situations that occurred to me. In addition to that I changed my actions. I subdued my pride in the face of humility. Further I practiced non-judgment and tried at all times to be generous with my time, my possessions, thoughts, words and abilities.

Finally I knew that life is as unique as the rainbow and that everyone experiences it differently. However, I came to understand that it was not the meaning of life, which was important, because every person has a different purpose and ultimately a unique plan in his existence. What mattered most was the feeling of life. Without realizing it, I had planted the precious seeds of the rainbow within me. It was important that the ethos of all these seven jewels were planted inside the hearts of man. Accidentally or otherwise I did that, together the precious jewels became a force within, a catalyst for change. I had now fulfilled the first two requirements Mami had mentioned. "Find the precious seeds and plant them."

Now remained just one element of Mami's allegory. "Be sure to nourish it." I stood as a bystander witnessing my own helplessness to be able to proceed any further. My rational mind could not conceive a way to surmount this last hurdle, yet in my surrender was the uncovering of the final sacrament. The awe-inspiring realization that divine love was the Nexus. It was indeed the very substance with which the Universal soul sustained creation.

At the Taj Mahal I experienced the real nature of this divine love. Love is the glue that holds the world together; it is the spring that nourishes the spirit in us. Without knowing it I nourished my innermost being, and the seven jewels of the rainbow within me were fed with love. Like the laws of gravity that moves objects, I emerged into my sacred space and was overcome and overwhelmed by the laws of the spirit Mami understood so well. In this I was thrust into a solitary encounter with the universal soul. In that ecstatic moment I bathed in its shimmering glory, tasted its nectar and experienced bliss, and like a caterpillar that became a butterfly, for a second I died before my time and yet lived to express the certainty of its love. Like the moth that was annihilated in the flame, I too was consumed in the universal soul. In that ephemeral, I experienced the transformation of my very essence and uncovered the feeling of life. Jonathan concluded that he had discovered the perennial truth and the wisdom of the ages forever sought by mankind. Any human beings who took these treasured seven jewels of the Rainbow and planted them into their own hearts in entirety, subsequently nourished them with the rapture of love, for them will be the reward of the alchemy of happiness. They will enact the laws of the spiritual realm with absolute certainty, which will forever transform and elevate them. In this will they witness the unraveling of the mystery called life, making it possible for them to scale the celestial apex, that zenith to which all human beings aspire.

Finally Jonathan came to know that the secret to humankind's happiness and enlightenment was given to the West and to the East. Such was the destiny of Jonathan and Dirum.

"What will you do when you get back to your family?" Jonathan asked, noticing they were nearing Delhi.

"Well, I am going to make some changes in my life, but above all I feel we have been given the wisdom for a reason, and I will discover the plan. What about you, my friend?" asked Dirum sincerely.

"The last few days I have felt Crystal call me. It's time for me to create unity in my family and fulfill the promises I have made. After that, I will allow the universal soul to show me how this wisdom can be planted in the hearts of people in the West," answered Jonathan confidently.

The train stopped at Delhi. This was to be the place where the two companions were to go their separate ways.

"I am terrible at goodbyes," said a melancholy Dirum.

"And I," said Jonathan as they embraced. They stood facing each other, holding hands. "I can see from your face that you have a poem for me."

"Yes, I do, the Persian poet, Jami, can say it better than I can," answered Dirum, as he gently recited this verse:

In proximity remains always
The dread of it passing
But in distance lies nothing
But hope for union.

The worthy emissaries parted company, one traveling to the East and the other to the West, carrying with them the wisdom of the ages.

Epilogue

FROM THE DIARY OF JONATHAN TSOL

Plant the jewels of the rainbow into your life...
Attain the wisdom of the ages,
and the secrets of everlasting happiness

For the few shiny beads of gold,
For the few trinkets of pleasure,
I clipped my wings to fit in a cage.[3]

*L*ike most people, I lived my life as if it was an emergency. With the masses, I drove along the highways of the consumer society, following the mantras of materialism. The rule was simple: strive to own as much as you can and happiness will follow. I played this game for the longest time, truly believing that the illusory state of material well-being was just around the corner. Little did I know that it was a circle from which I could not escape. The happiness and meaning I sought seemed a mirage in a plastic world where life was increasingly more of a burden than a blessing. I was suffocating in a prison I mistook for freedom. Ironically everyone seemed to have a clear idea of how other people should lead their lives but were unsure about their own.

Through a series of amazing coincidences, which I discovered later to be life's calling, I found myself in the northern areas of Pakistan, those legendary foothills of the Himalayas. There I realized that we live in a natural world, which is perfectly planned and ordered. From the smallest plant to the fiercest animal a harmony existed. This was also very evident in the signs of nature, the alternation of the sun, moon and the seasons, which changed like clockwork. I came to understand that nature was a language through which the sustainer talked and communicated with us on the exoteric plain. Yet man was the odd one out, always in contradiction and forever trying to adapt the world to himself.

It became apparent that we had forsaken our exalted status and shifted our center to our lower self. Thus we became humans who were accidentally and occasionally spiritual. Our inner solitude and outer humanity had been lost in the emergence of the techno-human being. I now understood why there was pain and anguish in the hearts of man who found happiness and meaning so illusive. We had become like a salmon forever struggling upstream.

Mami had become a guide who helped me understand that each human being occupied a scared space which we could discover by finding the Rainbow's real treasure. The metaphor of the Rainbow was unique and profound. It is formed by a multitude of single droplets of water differing in size. A single white ray of light reflected and refracted on these droplets gave cause to the rainbow. As a result of this, no two people ever see the same rainbow, even though they may stand beside each other. Everyone that we share our planet with sees a different rainbow. Similarly everyone's concept of happiness and meaning is also different! Therefore, instead of chasing someone else's idea of happiness and meaning, we needed to find our own.

After all, meaning and happiness are not homogenous products. They are not found on billboards, commercials and magazines, nor are they found in material things.

In this way the rainbow speaks to us, a kindred spirit to all who are in awe of its beauty and splendor. We can reach the metaphoric status of the Rainbow by planting its attributes into our lives and nourishing them with love. This enables us to journey to its source, that single white ray of light which originates from the Universal soul.

Mami taught me to know the greater meaning of life beyond our senses by helping me find my sacred space. Above all he trusted me with the wisdom of the ages, those seven jewels of the rainbow from the Akashic records. They were the alchemy of happiness. Plant them in your heart and nurture them with love, he told me, and I would discover the meaning of life and the secrets to everlasting happiness. I did this and in the process witnessed the transformation of my very essence during which I discovered the truths sought by man since the beginning of time. It is said that the greatest miracle of all is the one that allows a person to go from ignorance to wisdom. This then is the treasure of the Rainbow which adorns our skies.

As an emissary I bring this miracle to you. They are the seven jewels of the rainbow, the blueprints for the total approach to balanced living. Plant them in their entirety into your heart and let these seeds become the foundation of your code of conduct during this passage on earth. Furthermore, at each occasion nourish them with enduring love. In this endeavor you too will witness the reformation of your being. You will envision the real beyond the illusory world of our physical existence. It will heal you and lift your spirit, bringing lasting happiness and success. We are infinitely more than we think; if we only knew what our soul knows. The meaning of life and the wisdom of the ages, my friend, are now in the palms of your hands. The choice is yours.

Meditation

THE *GREEN* JEWEL OF THE RAINBOW

Mami had always reminded me that, he who knows himself, knows the universal soul. I learned very quickly that in this endeavor, meditation is the gateway. This was the only way to connect with the spark of the universal soul that exists in all man.

Meditation enables us to move beyond the mind. In this way we leave behind all the baggage and conditioning we have accumulated since our childhood.

The definition of meditation is "The dynamic retention of our awareness on a chosen subject or theme." The subject of meditation should be a lucid love and endless craving for the universal soul. Different people have different definitions for this universal soul. Some know him as god, the sustainer, the creator, the lord, the spirit, Rabb, Krishna, Allah. Others will identify him through their religion. Remember there are many names and numerous paths to the one truth.

Meditation is the first and perhaps the defining jewel because it connects us to the pulse of the universal soul. It is the very portal to the higher realm, and without meditation this journey cannot start. Retention of our awareness on this theme will require that you develop an ability to concentrate.

Concentration is the key to meditation. It is a word that originates from Latin, meaning something which has a common center, expressed as one pointedness. The average mind is filled with countless thoughts and therefore each one is weak. However, replacing all these useless thoughts with just one that we have chosen will give us the desired objective. This means that we must first dominate our minds. It is said, "He who masters his mind liberates his self." Mami used to say that the mind was like a wild horse that had to be tamed. In this conquest was the path to pure consciousness.

Concentration is then used as a rocket booster helping us transcend all the worldly thoughts to reach meditation where we sit in the silence of the mind contemplating a deep love for the creator and devoid of any material thought.

Meditation in this way should take place at the two ends of the day. Very early in the morning when the material world's influence is at the lowest ebb. Finally the last thing before sleeping for this will cleanse and purge the mind. This ensures that our connection to the Universal rhythm remains strong and that its light illuminates our path.

It is said that those who rule their mind rule the world. This is very true. You will discover that often the mind is rebellious and cannot be easily subdued. Nevertheless with will power and passion, you can penetrate the mind, and enter the realm of pure sprit.

There is a polish that taketh away rust and the polish of the soul within is meditation.

Relinquish Pride

THE *RED* JEWEL OF THE RAINBOW

*I*n my journey I came to understand that pride was a debasing element which binds man to his lower self. The ego in the human being has a big appetite.

Its food is haughtiness, because it has an over-exaggerated impression of its own self worth.

I know that in my own life, pride had become a mask through which anger and rage was expressed. It was born from a deep insecurity to cling to some misguided image of my own importance. This then had become an ailment, which drew me closer to the instinctive and animal nature of my lower self. In this way pride, rage and anger had become instruments of power like those of fire and bombs. The lesson I learnt was that those who use them seldom escape its wrath in their own lives. I could see that pride had become a screen and a barrier to the light of wisdom. After all, when we are full of ourselves we occupy that space into which the light of the universal soul should flow. The only way we can remove the anchors of pride that keep us shackled to the lower self is by becoming humble. Humility is a powerful strength that enables us to spread our wings. It recognizes that the proud mind is after all a created thing of the same substance as that of a tree, plants and soil. Humility draws us into our higher self—enabling growth and attracts the energy of the universal soul.

In all your expressions be mindful of the potential pride in us all. The strongest person is he who overcomes this vanity within. The red jewel of the Rainbow cannot manifest as long as there is even one rice grain of pride present.

Nonjudgment

THE *ORANGE* JEWEL OF THE RAINBOW

O ur judgments are based on the learnt knowledge of the world. What we learn from scholars and books does not give us wisdom of the greater knowledge. Furthermore, much of our perception and outlook is a product of our previous experiences including the conditioning, preconceptions and prejudices we inherit from a young age. How could we possibly make judgments about people's actions and their circumstances based on such shallow foundations?

I learnt that every human being is struggling to find his or her own path. In this way some are expressing their higher self whilst others are bound and mired to their lower self. Since each person has their own level of enlightenment, it is impossible to comprehend the status of another in this path we call life. Our attempts to be judgmental could be compared to the observations of someone lost in the desert and seeing water in the mirage.

Therefore our continual determinations and opinions validate the limited and illusory perceptions we have acquired and negate the existence of the greater wisdom. They thus become balls and chains binding us to the lower self.

There is a greater knowledge beyond that which we have learnt, and our pronouncements become deceptions through which we mislead others and ourselves. The orange jewel tells us that wisdom is the discovery of our own ignorance. Let us focus on our own path and avoid judging the action of others for in this we can raise the seat of our self to the higher realm.

Generosity

THE *YELLOW* JEWEL OF THE RAINBOW

Generosity is the disposition of the higher self. Mami taught me that our expressions to help others with our time, means and resources raises us. This, he said, was an indomitable spiritual truth.

The natural world that surrounds us provides ample evidence that everything in it gives and takes. If the oceans did not give up their water, would there be rain? If the seed was not sacrificed and planted, would there be trees, forests and fruit? The abundance of giving is apparent in all the signs of nature. Yet man is the only one who takes and hoards. Such selfish acts are at odds with the natural flow of energy and they draw man to his lower self. Life's message is painfully obvious; whenever we plant seeds the return is multiplied conforming to a spiritual principle.

In my time with Mami I came to understand that those who bring sunshine to the lives of others rarely keep it from themselves. Therefore, those who consider power and success as trophies to collect are missing life's great opportunity, which calls us to rise above the selfish nature of our lower being.

The inflow and outflow consistent within the physical world is a necessary aspect of its continual renewal. This happens with or without man's cooperation. All things are ultimately recycled including people's most valuable possessions. Death ensures this! However, the choice to participate in this virtue defines our character. If we can tell a tree by its fruits, then an enlightened man is known by his generosity and service to others. Therefore, all of us need to accept what life offers with gratitude, but we should also be willing to share a part of that which is in excess. Without this giving, man sinks into his lower self just like the dead sea stagnates without an outflow of water.

The path to the higher self, Mami once said, was in allowing the best in us to emerge. I have begun to understand that the best thing a human has is his ability to serve. Only man has the choice to help and touch people's lives, and it is this act of service that separates us from the animals. Therefore, serve generously for it is the highest form of giving. This will move us out of the animal in us to the spirit within, allowing us to step into the higher self.

So avoid selfishness, for it is a barrier to abundance. The yellow jewel manifests when we endeavor to help others get what they want for in this act is the prosperity we seek. It is better to light one candle, help one person, than to dream about changing the world.

Express Your Higher Self

THE *BLUE* JEWEL OF THE RAINBOW

During the journey, I came to understand the dual nature of the human being. The higher self, characterized by higher thinking; and the lower self, by the instincts of physical survival.

In order to flow within the light emanating from the universal soul, we have to center our life into the higher self. Therefore, the timeless ethics of kindness, tolerance, selflessness and forgiveness have to become a code of conduct. On the other hand, expressions of jealousy, envy, greed, anger, hatred, lust, arrogance, malice and the like were debasing expressions from the lower self which put us at odds with the universal soul. Ultimately such actions created a crust of ignorance around the mirror of the soul, harnessing us firmly in the world of the profane.

However, the knowledge that we have the power to control our responses is liberating, because we alone determine how high we soar. The way we respond to circumstances is the ticket to our ultimate freedom. Therefore, by centering our life on the higher self we are raising the seat of our consciousness from the physical domain of the finite to the infinite realm of the spirit.

So in each response, regardless of the situation or circumstance, express your highest self, for this is the path upon which all those enlightened, past and present, walk. Remember life will continue to prod and push you. With every passing day new situations will arise to try you. Yet know that the response it seeks is the emergence of the nobility residing in your highest self.

Life is a Lesson

THE *VIOLET* JEWEL OF THE RAINBOW

During the course of my encounter with Mami, he made me realize one fundamental truth, which changed my perspective about life, "that we are in the world but not from the world." I now understand life to be a journey to self-actualization. It was not to be shuffled through in self-pity; instead it was a unique opportunity to grow. Every adventure and circumstance presents in its midst important lessons that enable our development in this world.

In the same way that we build our physical muscles by training and giving them a load to carry, our spirits are strengthened through life's loads. It is the good and bad situations life prods us with that provide the opportunity to discover our true capacity. These are the moments when we are invited to be courageous and to respond with our highest self.

During our journey in this place called earth there are no mistakes, nor is there blame. The only thing that matters are the lessons we learn, for in them is our illumination. I remember reading Epictetus who wrote, "On the occasion of every accident that befalls you remember to turn to yourself and inquire what power you have for turning it to use."

The fact remains that this world is not a place of permanent settlement. It is a passage, a road upon which we travel towards eternity. Every breath we take is another step towards the inevitable, death. Yet, within each breath lies also an invincible life springing forth from within, calling us to grow with every experience.

All enlightened travelers see the trials and tribulations offered by life as opportunities to seek a deeper meaning. The seasons we witness are a natural part of the world we live in, from those seasons of beginnings to those of the end, from those in our environment to those above us in the celestial spheres. Similarly there are seasons in the finite passage of our lives. Those winters when we confront problems and pains to the summers when we count our blessings.

Therefore, in whatever personal season we are in at this time, whether it is the harsh reality of anguish, difficulties and problems to the coolness of the summer's breeze. These tough seasons never last, yet each one brings forth a new lesson, from which we grow and strengthen our spirit during our sojourn in this world. So learn the lesson in each day for fear that we may have to learn it again.

Discover Your Plan

THE *INDIGO* JEWEL OF THE RAINBOW

*T*he world is perfectly planned and balanced. The same water that nourishes the smallest plant and the largest mammal nurtures us too. As much as man struggles to assert his identity to adapt the world to himself, he is still bound by the same natural laws. What made us so different, I wondered, because after all, the reflection in the mirror competed fiercely for food and space with the other creatures we share the planet with.

I came to understand that the only thing that separates us is the spark of the universal soul prevalent in all human beings making them spiritual. This uniqueness is evident in the consciousness and freewill afforded only to man. This resides in the higher self and it is from here that all the nobler virtues endowed to man emanate.

There is a plan for everything in the perceptible and imperceptible world, this Mami confirmed. The discovery of our own mission, or purpose in life, puts us into harmony with the universal soul, which supports and sustains us at all times.

Whether we live in the East or the West, whether we are rich or poor, a doctor or farm worker, this hierarchy is limited to the material and finite world of our physical existence. Yet within our own circumstance and particular situation lies a destination and a personal plan. It is the discovery of this that leads inevitably to happiness. Though the seeds of our exhalted destiny exist within our grasp, alas they cannot be reached and plucked. Instead we have to center our life in the higher self, which will allow us to discern the language of the universal soul, recognize its pulse and enable us to walk in its flow. Inevitably the laws of the universe will conspire to reveal to us our personal plan.

Love

Why do you cry?
Why do you form a veil across my eyes,
Blurring the Beautiful Sight?[3]

There are many things in life, which are so obvious, yet often we are blind to them. This I came to understand with respect to the final piece I hungered for. I recalled a conversation with Mami whom I asked probingly about the real nature of the universal soul. "He was unique, above all and beyond imagination. Though he is known by the communities past and present with different names, there was only one reality whose language is love." Tell me more about this love I had asked. "Love manifests wherever the divine reality is contemplated for it is the fragrance of the infinite," Mami had assured me.

This love is indeed the glue that holds everything together, an eternal spring that nurtures the natural beauty and balance in our cosmos. Like the fish that went in search for water, we seek love, yet every second of our life we are submerged in its ceaseless flow. We just need to awaken to this realization for in this is our triumph.

I came to the realization that though the created world could not contain nor perceive the vastness of love radiating from the sustainer, the heart of a human in whom resided the seven jewels of the rainbow could, for it was the nexus. When we nourish the rainbow seeds within us with love, that nucleus of the supreme, we will witness a

ANIL GIGA

harvest unthinkable and an ascent unimaginable, which is our emergence from ignorance to enlightenment!

So express all the jewels of the rainbow, meditate; subdue pride; be non-judgmental; be generous; express your higher self; trust life as a lesson; discover your plan; with undying love, that agape which is selfless at all times. In this will the seven precious seeds bloom, surrendering to you the greatest treasure of all, the wisdom of the ages and the feeling of life. This is my prayer and your destiny.

References

(1) The Mathnawi of Jalalu'ddin Rumi.

(2) Rubaiyat of Omar Khayya'm.

(3) Gulshan Remtulla